GATHERINGS

MARINA RUST

Simon & Schuster
New York   London   Toronto
Sydney   Tokyo   Singapore

SIMON & SCHUSTER
Simon & Schuster Building
Rockefeller Center
1230 Avenue of the Americas
New York, New York 10020

SIMON & SCHUSTER and colophon are registered trademarks of
Simon & Schuster Inc.

DESIGNED BY BARBARA MARKS
Manufactured in the United States of America

10   9   8   7   6   5   4   3

Library of Congress Cataloging in Publication Data
Rust, Marina
      Gatherings : a novel / Marina Rust.
         p.   cm.
      I. Title.
   PS3568.U8127G38   1993
   813'.54—dc20   92-32354
                                           CIP

ISBN: 0-671-70315-3

FOR MY PARENTS

"We're the same people," he said, walking on the beach.
Knowing that we weren't, I asked, "How?"
"Because we've lost the same things."
It was not the answer I expected, but it pleased me.

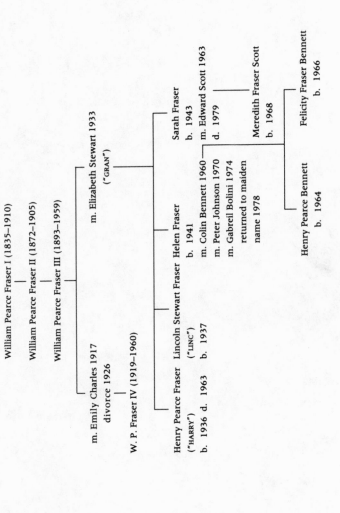

William Pearce Fraser I (1835–1910)

William Pearce Fraser II (1872–1905)

William Pearce Fraser III (1893–1959)

m. Elizabeth Stewart 1933
("GRAN")

m. Emily Charles 1917
divorce 1926

W. P. Fraser IV (1919–1960)

Henry Pearce Fraser   Lincoln Stewart Fraser   Helen Fraser
("HARRY")   ("LINC")   b. 1941
b. 1936 d. 1963   b. 1937   m. Colin Bennett 1960
                                                              m. Peter Johnson 1970
                                                              m. Gabreil Bolini 1974
                                                              returned to maiden
                                                              name 1978

Sarah Fraser
b. 1943
m. Edward Scott 1963
d. 1979

Meredith Fraser Scott
b. 1968

Henry Pearce Bennett
b. 1964

Felicity Fraser Bennett
b. 1966

Beaufort, South Carolina,
July 1990

The town bookshop is open late. Eleanor, the owner, is the first friend I've made in town.

Most days, I stop by the shop on my walk home from the newspaper office. By six the edge is off the heat, but people still move slowly. By seven Bay Street is empty; locked whitewashed storefronts shine with late watery light from the harbor.

The bookstore is small, but bright with pine. Eleanor puts the new arrivals on a special shelf.

Tonight I pick up a book of Swedish fairy tales, thick with color plates. "It's really for adults," Eleanor says, as I look at the price. "Some of the illustrations would frighten children."

Fairy tales can be too dark, too savage, for children. Think of Hansel and Gretel. Witches lurk, waiting to cage and fatten children.

My mother wouldn't read me fairy tales, but not because she thought they'd frighten me. Back then I didn't scare easily.

But if she didn't read them to me, I wonder how I came to know the stories: princesses in towers, dragons in moats, knights in silver.

From the start I was familiar with these things. What nobody tells us we make up for ourselves.

EARLY
ON

South Carolina

The only time my mother took me to Heyton Hall was Easter of '74. We were there for Aunt Helen's garden wedding—a small one, her third, a Mr. Bolini.

Cousin Felicity, age seven, clutched a small nosegay, a look of adult displeasure on her face.

Cousin Henry Pearce, nine, stood in a short grey suit with hands clasped behind him as he rocked back and forth, crushing the grass.

Aunt Helen took her vows in a pink A-line dress, then, after cake, changed into a peacock-blue suit with white gloves in which to go away, leaving her children behind.

Easter morning Gran arranged an egg hunt. Colored

eggs lay scattered across the lawns and gardens—half hidden at the base of an oak, at the heart of a boxwood, cradled in the arms of a green oxide nymph.

Henry Pearce and Felicity hunted separately, competitively. I followed them across the brilliant lawn, freshly clipped. Gran's lawns were ryegrass, seeded in the fall and magically green through the winter. Not like the grass I knew out west, which, even in summer, grew patchy at best.

The three of us searched the pond's shaded banks, the edge of the clear dark water. Further out, the pond reflected sunlight, a duck paddled undisturbed.

Three feet up, against the bank, I saw something half submerged, black and shiny. The thick top of a curve, a bicycle tire. Another step, and I froze.

The black scales rolled like rope as the serpent returned to the water. It slid quickly, evenly—with a gentle plop, no splash. The only sound then was the beating of my heart.

"Did you know there were snakes in there?" I asked my cousins. They nodded.

Water moccasins had always lived in the pond, and along the banks you had to be brave.

January 1980

My next visit to Heyton Hall was six years later, after my mother had died.

By this time Henry Pearce was just "Pearce." My aunt had named him for our uncle Harry. But Harry had died, and Helen's friends thought it morbid to call her baby boy that, so for a while he was saddled with the full "Henry Pearce," a real rock of a name. He shortened it when he went away to school, easier for the other boys, who could be quite cruel.

Pearce was—and would remain—lightly tanned, suggesting labor neither indoors nor out. He clipped his words cleanly in tones not quite English, not quite American.

Coming down to dinner he wore his head wet—sleek and small and glossy. I remember thinking he had a head like a seal.

After dinner we'd play cards—Go Fish until he taught me solitaire.

August 1982

The Maine beaches were like those out west—grey pebbled coves flanked by boulders. Dark rocks jutted out of grassy lawns that rolled down from Helen's white porches and rose garden.

Cousin Pearce wore turtlenecks and a rope bracelet that summer. I remember the bracelet on his wrist as we sat on those boulders in late afternoon light. He held a cigarette, which he rarely took breath from. Later he would give up smoking, saying that it was killing his tennis. He squinted in the sun, and his hair—not slicked this time—hung in a short clean curtain, straight and gleaming.

Pearce played with the laces of my white canvas Keds, slowly looping a string from each shoe into a gentle knot. I watched, fascinated, as his hands—well formed and unmarked—pulled to finish the work.

"Untie me," I said, pushing my toe against the boulder.

Pearce, cross-legged, looked up, intent. He took the cigarette from between his lips and tapped its tip against

15

his loafer, ashes falling into the cuff of his pale pressed chinos.

"Untie me," I repeated.

He turned his attention back to my laces.

Slowly, he took the glowing end of his cigarette and pressed it onto the white string, near the knot.

When he lifted it the string was blackened, frayed, but holding.

"Untie me," I said, my voice low.

He took both my hands. At first I tried to pull them back. He smiled. He didn't let go.

Without a word he guided my hands down my leg to my ankles, placed both upon the laces.

"Pull," he said.

I did. The string broke clean.

Aunt Helen drove me to Connecticut for school that next week.

I was not as nervous as I could have been. There were the new clothes, Helen's Volvo, and Aunt Helen herself at the welcoming tea in silk twill trousers, pearls, French cuffs.

This is when I started to see more of them—my mother's family. It had become geographically feasible and, in my aunt's words, about time.

PART I

WINTER
PICNIC

**Heyton Hall, South Carolina,
January 1983**

Uncle Linc settles back in the canvas director's chair with his Scotch. The breeze picks up from the marsh as he begins another one of his hunting stories; this one about his '62 safari with Uncle Harry, the year before he died.

". . . And so Harry'd told our guide he'd take the Land-Rover and drive it all the way back to Nairobi himself . . . wanted to make it back in time for some god-awful embassy Christmas dance." Linc pauses, considering. "He wouldn't really have *done it*, you know, but the idea of Harry loose on the plains scared those people so that they ditched the shoot, rounded up someone else's truck. . . . People'd do anything for Harry. . . ."

I, for one, like listening to Uncle Linc's stories. Linc has the family voice—a voice that puzzles people, since really none of us are English. But then there are some added bits in Linc's voice that sound Southern, which makes sense since he's down in South Carolina with Gran much of the winter. Gran, of course, has never gotten to sound Southern. She just hasn't met many Southerners. But then again, if she had, they'd probably end up sounding more like her, not she like them.

Gilbert hasn't finished serving, but Gran begins eating. I hesitate, looking from her down to the roasted dove. I pick up my knife and fork and begin to saw tiny slivers of flesh from the bone.

"And that night Harry pulled a helluva trick on our guide—almost got himself shot! He had, as you can imagine, quite a few after dinner, and that Masai sun must have gotten to him during the day—he was always hatless. Well, naturally, in this state, nothing struck him as funnier than the deep snuffling sounds made by the Cape buffalo." Linc demonstrates, snorting air deep in his throat. "So Harry, being pretty damn good with imitations, practices that god-awful sound after lights in our tent—thought it was great!" Linc laughs, almost choking. "So then he wanders over to the poor guide's tent and tries it there, lowing and mooing just outside the flaps. Certainly must've done one helluva job—guide almost shot out into the darkness with an elephant rifle. Poor man told us later that Harry had managed to imitate a *wounded* bull!" Linc's voice trails off as he looks around the table, waiting for a reaction. He turns to Gran. "You see, Mum, there's nothing near so dangerous—they have horns four feet 'cross." He spreads his arms wide. "And that sound . . ."

"Mmm," says Gran, busy with her bird.

Bending back in his chair, Linc yawns and stretches, crossing his hands behind his neck. "Trust Harry to do just the wrong thing so well. . . ." He laughs alone for a moment, then, distracted, fans at the smoke that's drifted over from the cooking pit. "Mum, could Gilbert move the table? Wind's changed direction."

Gran looks up. "And will again! Really, now. The rest of us are fine." She turns to Pearce and begins telling him something about land taxes.

"Smoke hurts my eyes," grumbles Linc as he rips a tiny brown leg from his dove. He inserts the little limb between his teeth, then, yanking hard, strips it completely. Elbows on the table, he holds the bone up between thumb and forefinger, examining it. I glance over to Gran. Having long given up on her son's table manners, she's begun her salad.

The sun beats warm on our sweaters and faces, although the air is cool. Linc's audience has dwindled to the three of us for this afternoon's picnic. Aunt Helen's left for Florida, Felicity for school.

Far Point is a good drive from the main house, a good place for a picnic. Come February, with camellias blossoming in their full range of pinks and creams, the gardens will—in their more obvious way—invite. But on January afternoons the wide plains along the marsh reign starkly beautiful.

This is the view from our picnic table: earth and sky stretching along a low flat horizon, the line interrupted once by a blackened tree trunk. Warm light turns the brown grass gold, the sky appears bluer in contrast. One would not think the landscape dead, or even slumbering, on these immensely quiet, cool, and bright afternoons.

The silence is broken by the caw of a crow. Pearce's eyes follow the bird as it swoops over the water. The sunlight catches the high symmetry of his face, lashes glinting gold.

Pearce had stayed on for the shooting. It surprised me that he'd miss the New York parties. Every evening around five the phone would start to ring, then Gilbert would walk slowly into the living room, where we'd be finishing tea. He'd bow his head slightly: "Telephone for Mr. Pearce." Pearce would hang on the phone for hours, busy with people asking him to come up. Cousin Felicity says that Pearce has only been so attentive to family because a year ago Gran called him on the carpet. Mrs. Hellman had sent her a gossip clipping from the *Daily News*, chronicling a Guy Fawkes party Pearce had given at a nightclub which brought the fire department and heavy water damage. Gran was livid, but eventually both she and Pearce settled down. Or, at least, appeared to. Pearce had, Uncle Linc explains, all the charm that was Harry's, "and God knows Harry could charm any viper."

Strips of flesh dangle from the bone as Linc points it toward me:

"I don't see why Meredith here can't learn to shoot."

Neither Pearce nor Gran looks up.

"Sarah was a *great* shot—why, Meredith," he says, turning to me, "your uncle Harry and I took your mother out from the day she could lift the gun. She was so small, she had to use this little four-ten popgun. Even when she got bigger she'd use that four-ten. Well, one weekend 'round fifty-eight, Teddy Banes was down and the four of us were in the blinds after duck. Sarah was maybe seventeen at the time, but, like I said, she looked like a kid.

Well, Teddy says to your mother, 'Now, honey, you just point and shoot at those birds and I'll do the same, and then when one falls we'll tell your brothers you hit it.' Well, Sarah, she'd wait for him to take his shot. When he'd miss she'd fire, and the birds fell like rain. Teddy, he was steamed as hell, thought we'd set him up. Harry laughed his head off. Sarah, she looked like a kid, no older than Meredith here. . . ."

"Ow!" I bite down on something hard.

Pearce looks up. "Find a pellet?"

I wait until Pearce looks away before removing the small metal ball from my mouth, hiding it in my napkin. Linc continues:

"Lamont could teach you to shoot. You know Lamont, down at the barn. Must have been Lamont who taught your mother to shoot. We'll start you on clay tomorrow. You'll do great—should come easy as falling off a horse."

"She did that yesterday," says Pearce, in good humor.

I wince but answer Linc:

"That's awfully nice, but I'm leaving tomorrow."

"Next time, then. . . ."

I pause. "About my mother . . . She shot? I didn't think she liked guns."

Linc looks back in astonishment. "Sarah? Nonsense! Can't imagine it." He folds his arms behind his head, leans back in the chair. "Well, unless of course that was one of those things she decided once she went odd . . ."

Gran raises her eyes from her bird.

"Lincoln?"

"Yes, Mum?"

"If Meredith doesn't want to learn to shoot, we needn't force her."

"Yes, Mum."

. . .

Gilbert clears the coffee cups and Linc rises, pushing
with both hands against the arms of the chair to lift his
solid frame from the seat. He yawns and stretches, like a
bear after hibernation. Then he belches. Gran, selectively
deaf, doesn't hear. Pearce, looking the other way, pretends
not to notice. Gilbert clears the last saucer from the table.

I ride back in the Buick with my cousin and Linc. The
plantation roads are packed sand flanked with tall, evenly
spaced scrub pine. The pinewoods alternate with fields of
dry grass grown high. These are bird strips, patches of cover
carefully maintained.

Pearce and Linc are heading to the stables, dropping
me at the main house on the way. Pearce drives, as Gran
doesn't let Linc. Pearce has temporarily lost his license,
but that's all right so long as we stay on our own roads.
Linc's in front, next to his nephew; he rolls the window
down and rests his elbow on the sill, gesturing with that
hand.

"Now, we kids, we were welcome to risk our necks
any damn way we pleased, except with guns. Your grandfather, now, he made sure we were safe shots, had a thing
about it 'cause, you know, he heard the shot when his
own father shot himself."

I look up. "Great-Grandfather *shot* himself?"

"Cleaning the gun," says Linc over his shoulder.
"Made it look like an accident. At least to the Chicago
police."

Leaning forward from the back seat, I look to Pearce.
No reaction.

"But in those days," says Linc, "the Chicago police
were awfully polite. What else were they going to say?
Regardless, your grandfather—he was ten—he had been
in the nursery when he heard the shot. So he was always

24

very careful, made us kids unload our cartridges before crossing fences, that sort of thing."

"Sounds like good advice," I say.

"Unloading's not necessary if the pin's not cocked," says Pearce.

Linc continues. "I remember a big shoot up at Broadhurst. The governor was up; everyone knew he was an awful shot. Joke was that Father's pheasant were safe but we weren't sure about everybody else. Well, after the governor fires his first round, Harry walks right up and says, 'Adlai, if you're going to shoot someone, please shoot a houseguest. Houseguests we can get more of, but a good beater is hard to find—' "

Pearce interrupts. "I thought Harry said that to Mr. Dillon."

"Nope; Adlai. Mr. Dillon was a perfectly good shot. Anyway, I thought your grandfather was going to bust a blood vessel, but he laughed it off. But we *had* been taught to be careful with guns."

"I wish I'd known Harry," I say.

I hear a sigh—an actual sigh—from Linc. "Yes, you would have liked Harry . . . everyone did." The car passes over a bump, and I hear something scrape bottom. Linc taps the ashes of his cigarette out the window before turning to Pearce: "You hear Gran refer to you as 'Harry' the other night?"

"She's old," says Pearce, after a moment.

Linc continues. "Myself, I could never have been like Harry, though I s'pose I wanted to. Could never get away with as much. He'd just smile that way, say just the thing and that was that. . . . Harry made everyone like him." Linc pauses. "Charming son-of-a-bitch." He draws from the cigarette and gazes out the window.

Pearce stares down the center of the road.

Linc goes on to tell a story of why there are no more Frasers at Groton.

". . . So Harry let the skunk loose in the heating vent! No one could go into that chapel for days!" Then Linc's voice softens. "Yeah, he got away with almost everything."

The silence that follows lasts until we reach the main gate. Linc gazes out the passenger's side to the long allée of oaks. Pearce, still looking straight ahead, quietly asks, "Shall I drop you here or at the house?"

"Here's just fine," I assure him, hopping out, glad to be back in the sunshine. The car continues down the road, raising two lines of dust.

———

My mother married two months after her brother's death, married a man she'd only just met, a man desperately in love with her. "I just had to get out of the house," she said.

There were many houses. There was Broadhurst, on Long Island's north shore, Grandfather's conception and pride. But Broadhurst had been closed up since Grandfather's death in '59. Like many big estates of its time, it was too expensive to keep up. The house and the land around it was sold to the Park Service to avoid subdivision. But there were still Stewart Cottage in Maine, the Seventy-second Street duplex, Heyton Hall for the winter.

I'd have thought my mother loved these houses. At least the ones in the country, the ones with stables. But what she said was that she had to get away.

My mother went to New York for Harry's funeral. The next day she was called in to the lawyer's office. He'd been crazy about Grandaddy.

"Your mother's planning a trip to Europe," he said. *"Where she'll be staying indefinitely. It's quite a blow she's taken, and she would very much like you to accompany her."*

"Sir, I can't. I'm getting married."

Later that night was the first my father ever heard of it.

———

Gran decorated both the living room and the gun room at Heyton Hall. The living room's all pale chintzes, butter cream with faded rose, blues and greens. Feminine, but not the fussy sort of feminine where a man would feel uncomfortable. There's a cultivated coziness, the sort where you can sink into a chair and get lost.

The gun room is located just before the living room, off the main hall. Gran must have meant it as Grandfather's retreat—an office for rare and happy shooting holidays. Grandfather died before I was born, but I feel I know him from that room. The walls are unfinished wood, dark and warm. One wall holds Audubon sketches of dove, geese, and quail. On another hangs a huge pen-and-ink map of the property in 1937. According to the box in the lower right-hand corner, the acreage was over sixteen thousand then. Less now. In the center of the room sits the largest desk I've ever seen—heavy, dark battered oak with brass fixtures. Across this lies an ancient green blotter, a black dial telephone, a low lamp.

This afternoon I'm sitting on the love seat, in the corner beside the bookshelf. On the shelf stands a row of photo albums—crimson leather stamped in gold.

I've leafed through these albums each visit, looking at now familiar names and dates sporadically marked on thick grey pages. Many of the photos are of picnics such as today's, but Gilbert is younger, has two men helping him.

When the children appear in the albums it is for holidays—Christmas or Easter.

There are a few trips. There's a group photo of the family lined up before the gangway of a ship. My mother and Helen stand small and neat in round-collared Peck & Peck suits, their dark hair neatly combed, caught and invisibly pinned to one side. The boys, taller, bob their heads, looking pleased but sheepish, too old for this. Gran and Grandaddy smile big—they're used to cameras.

The last album lies open in my lap. A black-and-white five-by-seven is centered alone on the page. Underneath, in Gran's hand: "Kenya 1962—The Boys."

Harry stands straight and tall, rifle in hand, in front of a canvas tent. He wears a white broadcloth shirt open at the neck; his legs are clad in khaki jodhpurs and tall polished riding boots. The hand without the gun is raised to his forehead; long, elegant fingers push back sun-streaked bangs, and he squints, smiling. A younger Linc stands, squared off and stern-looking, to his left. The albums end with this year.

Footsteps. I look up. Pearce, still in riding clothes, enters. We exchange nods. He walks out toward the living room, returns a minute later with a drink. He sits down next to me, long boot-clad legs stretched across the floor.

"Looking at the albums?"

I nod again, yes. Somehow I feel as if I've been caught at something wrong.

He looks down at the open book, the last photo.

"I've always liked that shot."

"It's a nice one," I answer.

"Have you been to East Africa?"

"No, never—"

"No, of course not. Good trip. Mum and I went when I was ten."

"Did you stay in tents like—"

"No. It was just a photo safari with these Austrian friends of Mum's. Hotels with pools, all that. It was O.K., but I'd like to go back, do it right."

"You should."

"It's changed."

"I'm sure. . . ."

We pause, turning our attention back to the photo.

"So . . . tell me," says Pearce. "Do you think Uncle Harry and I look so much alike?"

"It's hard to tell with black-and-white photos." I look up at Pearce, then down again. "Maybe a little around the jaw. And the eyes."

"The hair's different," says Pearce, running a hand over his.

"Uh-huh."

"But I've seen photos where he waters it."

"Waters it?"

"Slicks it. Like mine."

"Yes . . ."

Pearce takes a long sip and sits back in the love seat, squashing the pillows. The ice clinks in his glass. Then, lightly:

"Your mother was in love with him, wasn't she?"

"Excuse me?"

"Harry," he says. "Your mother was in love with him. . . ."

I just stare. Pearce shakes his head.

"No, no—I don't mean like *that*. What I mean is that she never got over him."

29

"I don't know. She never talked about him."

"I know. Neither does mine."

I don't know what to say.

Pearce takes another drink. His free arm rests at the side of the sofa, hand dangling limp as he regards the far wall, the empty gun cabinets.

———

My mother did once talk about Harry. We were living in Oregon; I was maybe eight. Mama had invited new people into the downstairs of the farmhouse, so she and I had moved into the attic. Our two rooms were really one, curtained off, a cotton ticking mattress on the floor for me.

One night I couldn't sleep. I reached for my red flashlight, stepped over the comic books and clothes strewn across the bare wood floor. Quietly, I parted the curtain. I could hear breathing from Mama's bed, slow and deep.

"Meredith?" I heard faintly.

"Yes."

"What's wrong?"

I followed the flashlight beam across to her bed, sat on the edge. "I can't sleep."

"Oh, no," she said, her voice faint, as if she'd been drugged and was waiting for the pill to take effect. She lifted a hand to stroke my hair. "Baby, you're too young for this."

"Tell me a fairy story."

"I don't know any fairy stories. . . ."

"Then tell me a story from when you were little."

Stroking my hair, she spoke quietly, her eyes closed.

She described two young girls at night looking out a window onto silver marshes, the moon lying flat, the reeds still and calm.

"He was on the porch. He was sad. . . ." Her voice was fading.

"Who?"

"The boy . . ."

"What boy?"

"Silly . . . never . . . what to say . . ."

I was eight and had never seen a picture of Harry, but I'm sure I knew him then. Closing my eyes, I could see the house and the porch, and then I could see him—the back of his head still and gleaming in moonlight, his hands clasped on his knees above the sharp crease of white flannel. I knew these things then in the same way I know now that his eyes were green, although all of the photos are in black and white.

But I whispered then to Mama: "What boy? Why was he sad?"

"Baby . . . try to sleep."

Her hand fell softly to her side. I knew not to wake her.

———

Framed, on the gun room wall:

A FATHER'S ADVICE

If a sportsman true you'd be,
Listen carefully to me.

If 'twixt you and neighboring gun
Bird may fly or beast may run,
Let this maxim e'er be thine:
FOLLOW NOT ACROSS THE LINE.

Stops and beaters oft unseen
Lurk behind some leafy screen;

31

Calm and steady always be:
NEVER SHOOT WHERE YOU CAN'T
SEE.

You may kill or you may miss
But at all times think of this—
All the quail ever bred
Won't repay for one man DEAD.

AT

BARBARA'S

Avon, Connecticut, March 1983

Barbara and I sit at the long pine table of her farmhouse kitchen, eating soup with thick slices of bread.

"Is Gilbert still there?" she asks.

I nod.

"Must be nearly seventy years old." Barbara Prewitt was my mother's best friend since Chapin and had spent holidays at Heyton Hall and Broadhurst. "Your mother and Helen were so isolated," she'd explained. "I'd be invited to stay for weeks—some attempt to make their fairy tale more normal."

Barbara lives now with her husband on a three-acre farm, raising ducks and rabbits, writing books. She's just half an hour from school, and at first I thought she'd sign me out for dinner just to be nice, but then I got used to the idea that she simply was nice. Anyway, it was wonderful on Saturdays when Barbara would pull up in front of the dorm, station wagon and cardigan sweater, just like the other girls' mothers.

"And Chessy?"

I nod again, mouth full.

"Does she still make plantation pie?"

"Sort of like pecan pie, but with raisins and things?"

"Yes, that."

I nod. Barbara smiles, lifts a bottle to pour.

I level my hand at the glass. "I'm not allowed wine on a dinner permission."

"Oh, for heaven's sake, you sound just like your mother." Barbara pauses. "So you're going down again for Easter?"

"I think so."

"Your father doesn't mind you spending all your vacations down there?"

"I guess not. California's kind of a haul."

"I suppose he enjoyed Heyton Hall too."

I nod.

I ask Barbara about the games, games I've heard were played.

"Well, there were two varieties. The safe and indoor—cards and charades—and the outdoor."

"What are those?"

"Your grandfather and the boys thought them up. Races, paperchases. That family went to the damndest lengths to hurt themselves. When I finally broke my collarbone I was proud because it seemed I'd joined the club."

"Pearce said he'd take me on a rattlesnake hunt."

"Tame. An afternoon ride through the woods."

34

"Not dangerous?"

"No. Rattlesnakes sleep in the sun. It's the water-moccasins you have to watch for. They hide."

Yes, I remember. "I stay away from the pond."

Barbara nods, then carefully: "How's your uncle Linc?"

"Fine."

"Quit his job yet?"

"No."

She seems on the verge of asking something, but doesn't.

"But he is spending a lot of time at Heyton Hall. He's talking about putting in shrimp tanks."

"Yes, your grandfather had that idea too—making the plantation self-supporting. But it could never be done."

"Why not?"

"Just the maintenance is incredible. Late every spring, crews would burn the bird strips, to kill the undergrowth so it wouldn't grow too high for the hunters. Thousands of acres to burn each year, a few strips at a time."

I nod, then pause. "Papa said that with Grandfather's politics, owning a plantation seemed contradictory."

"Well, there were a lot of contradictions in your grandfather."

———

From Eton, my grandfather kept two things: his accent and his ideals. He was an American businessman, but with a gentleman's voice and pre-war notion of honor between peoples and nations. It was a privileged notion for a smaller world.

He was not blind to change. When the depression came he turned New Dealer. Supported Roosevelt, the WPA, all of that. That's when he moved into newspapers.

The papers lost money, but he saw them as his good work, his contribution, giving the people their voice. It was an honorable life.

———

"My dad was a sturdy Republican," Barbara explains, rinsing dishes as I clear. "So I concluded that being a Democrat was very glamorous indeed. Dad was afraid I'd pick up strange ideas while lolling 'round Broadhurst or Heyton Hall. Really get frustrated. Heyton Hall bothered him particarly. He'd demand 'How can William Fraser lecture the rest of the nation about Negro rights when he keeps a plantation full of slaves?' I'd argue back, 'They're not slaves, Daddy, he pays them,' But then my father would ask, 'How do they live? Have you seen where they live?' and I'd keep silent, knowing that they lived in one-room shacks that we children passed while riding paper chases down the uglier roads of the property. There were a few things I didn't tell Dad about: the tin shacks and the watermoccasins."

———

There are things you half know, stories you've heard, points that sharpen like pencils when you hear them again. . . .

My mother didn't go back to Heyton Hall the spring she was pregnant. She used the morning sickness as her excuse, as she would for the rest of her term. That fall when Mama went into labor, Aunt Helen broke her promise and called Gran, who flew out from New York the next morning. There Gran was, not only in California of all terrible places, but in some large and dreadful hospital, there to claim her daughter and granddaughter. Mama wouldn't see her. Begging weakness, my mother told the nurse that she would receive no visitors except my father. Eventually, with my father's help, Gran got in. Mama and she had a polite chat; after five minutes Mama said she was tired, so Gran excused herself. Gran then charmed the clerk in charge of these things and had "Fraser" put on the birth certificate as my middle name.

For years I didn't know I had a middle name. I was eight when I discovered my birth certificate, stuck deep in a drawer. I showed it to my mother. "You don't need a middle name, sweetheart. Not everyone has to have a middle name."

"It's who I am, isn't it?" I said. She didn't answer.

———

Barbara tells me she wants me to understand some things. So that I can forgive my mother. For what, I'm not sure.

"For keeping me away?" I ask.

"In her eyes, keeping you safe."

SUMMER GAMES

Maine, August 1983

There is light fog, quiet and damp. The view out to sea is gentle grey. Down on the beach, workers prepare the cooking pits for tonight's clambake; the smell of coal smoke and cut grass drifts up the hill.

Stewart Cottage is turn-of-the-century colonial-revival clapboard. The doorways are arched and topped with fanlights, attic dormers jut from the roof. Long white porches wrap around two sides of the house, high Doric columns frame the view to the sea, the other islands.

Pearce—still in tennis whites—paces the porch, both hands tucked into the back waistband of his shorts. Stella, the housekeeper born on this island, walks out with a silver sailing cup holding a low arrangement of pink garden roses, yellow snapdragons, and blue delphiniums, which she places on a low glass-topped white wicker table.

Pearce picks up the cup and reads the inscription aloud.

" 'Twenties Class . . . 1947.' Stella, we're not doing well here. The Owens are coming tonight, and what do we have on the table? Nineteen forty-seven."

"Perhaps the Owens were away that year." Stella can joke with Pearce.

"I know what I need," Pearce says. "I need you to crew for me, that's what I need."

Stella laughs. "Oh, I'd weigh you down."

"No, we'd win absolutely. But then the Owens would of course hire you away from us, and we'd be back to losing races. Not to mention your angel food cake."

It is an island of friendly rivalries: the summer people versus the winterized, the sailors versus the golfers, the old families versus the new.

Many of the families have been coming to the island since the 1890s. Stewart Cottage was Gran's grandmother's then, its gabled roof and porches going up in six months and using all the island's laborers.

Gran still comes up for a week or so each summer, but officially she's sold the house to Aunt Helen, "Helen being the one with the large brood."

The telephone list for the island is a single double-sided page. A ferry brings out day-trippers—they bicycle along the main road, not finding much, and return to the mainland before dark. The island's pleasures are well hidden, tucked tight among the pines.

Across the bay, you can barely see the yacht club—a small grey clapboard box with white trim, a low porch, and a shingle roof. The club dock has but one float, dinghies and whalers bobbing. A few substantial yachts and a scattering of turnabouts lie anchored in the bay. This is the view from Aunt Helen's. If there's no fog.

The adults of this gentle curve of the island gather for drinks at seven. They stand in sweaters and blazers on Helen's porch with one arm wrapped snug around their waist, hand tucked under an elbow. The other hand juts out, gripping a fresh napkin and a short glass.

Mrs. Owen's drink arm bobs slightly as she makes a point.

"... *Weekly* tennis tournaments. Round robin and elimination. An *excellent* sailing clinic ..."

Mrs. Owen is a lean, hard-edged blond, recently back from visiting her sister in Newport. Three days at Bailey's Beach has lent new fervor to her favorite peeve—our club's poorly organized junior sports.

Aunt Helen gracefully ducks out of Mrs. Owen's circle to greet white-haired Mrs. Atcheson at the porch doorway. Mrs. Atcheson's voice booms over. "Helen dear, you're looking *lovely*. But aren't you *freezing*?"

"Not a bit." Aunt Helen does a full catwalk turn, white arms to the side like a ballerina. "Temperature's all in the head." Helen's fuchsia raw-silk sheath is cap sleeved and mandarin collared, made expressly for her in Hong Kong.

The island scene is divided into two groups: the Adults and the Young. All those—including the marrieds—between twelve and forty consider themselves the Young, there being far too few to break into subsets. There is a small, late party every night during those key three weeks in August. Usually at the Christophers' boathouse, out of earshot of the main house, where Mr. and Mrs. Christopher lie asleep, snug and happy in the knowledge that their sons won't be driving.

But seven o'clock's for adults. Mrs. Owen continues.

"Tennis clinics in the morning, Mercury races in the afternoon. Keeps kids out of trouble all day, *and* away from the snack bar."

"But their club is bigger," protests Amanda Lowe, a young married in a black turtleneck, not so far herself from lazy afternoons floating aimlessly in a ski boat. The older woman talks of summer teams and Labor Day award dinners. The younger points out fierce family sailing rivalries where the losers buy the winners sugar cones with chocolate jimmies.

Mrs. Owen says that she does not consider the Tuesday-Thursday races the same as really organized activity.

"And it seems," she continues, "that all these kids *do* these days is sit around The Island Store for hours on end, running up ice cream bills. Four hundred dollars in ice cream alone last summer! And do tell, what's become of the mother-daughter round-robins?"

Aunt Helen, who's been circulating, dips back into the circle and beams at Mrs. Owen.

"So what are we all talking about?"

Beyond the lamplight of the porch, down on the rocks, a group of kids has gathered. They're sunburned red but huddle shivering against the wind, ducking their noses into the gaping necks of Bean sweaters and drawing knees up tight against their chests. They perch just above the high-water mark, their hands cold white, clutching bottles of St. Pauli Girl. The ages go from fourteen or so up to cousin Felicity, who's taking courses at Penn part time

41

while she runs a stable. The youngest of the Christopher brothers—skinny, with a deep burn and shaggy white-blond hair like the rest of them—has been playing with Felicity's braid, slipping off the elastic, undoing the long plait, doing it back up again. He gives a tug when he's finished, and Felicity reaches back to check the job.

Mrs. Owen asks if I play tennis.

"Not well, I'm afraid."

Mrs. Owen takes this as fact. "I'm sure you *could* play good tennis, if you worked on it. Your mother was so good, you know."

"No. I didn't know."

"Very competitive. Fought for every shot."

I think of my mother—hushed tones and passive resistance—and can't imagine her arguing line calls.

I say to Mrs. Owen, "But she was a good sport, wasn't she?"

"How do you mean?"

"Well, what would happen when she lost a match?"

"I wouldn't know. She didn't."

Felicity stands up, resting her can of 7-Up on a flat span of rock. The youngest Christopher stands too—they're skipping stones, having a contest. The others crouch amid the boulders, searching for flat thin stones. Timing is important—it's not easy, like on a duck pond. You have to flick the stone so as to catch the wave as it recedes, leaving a long, flat trail of water. But sometimes an incoming wave will surprise you, catching your stone at its tip and sending it sailing farther than you'd hoped. But generally these land with a heavy plop, sinking straight.

42

Gordon Emerson stands next to me on the rail. He's watching Felicity too.

"You see, she's using her wrist, not her elbow," he says, balancing Brie on a cracker and a glass of ginger ale. Gordon wears a narrow striped bow tie and arrived with his mother. Helen had made a big show of introducing us—"You two must be about the same age!"

Nearby, Pearce entertains a few of the younger wives.

"My sister won't talk to anyone who's over twelve or hasn't got hoofed feet," he's saying. "She ought to start charging you all fifty cents an hour for baby-sitting." He nods toward me. "Look: even Meredith can stand up here and behave like a grownup."

Gordon asks, "Do you know if Felicity's going to the Christophers' tonight?"

I shake my head.

Mrs. Owen's voice drifts over from the darkening porch.

"We really should form a committee to evaluate the club's junior games."

There's a whoop from the rocks as Felicity's stone sinks, a row of seven rings fading in the water behind.

The next week it rains steadily. People retreat to far corners of the house. Pearce and Billy Lowe find an old game of Pong; faint electronic blips and cries of victory float down from the attic.

We see less of Helen. She arranges no dinners and declines invitations. She appears to spend the day sleeping—her bedroom door remains closed.

Last night I heard Felicity at her mother's door. "You're awake; I can see your light," Felicity called through the wood. I could not hear Helen's response.

This morning I pad around carefully, staying out of sight. I shop for a book in the study. It's not really a study, but it's where Aunt Helen keeps her desk—stationery, pens, rolls of Life Savers candy stuck in the pigeonholes. The curtains—heavy dark brocade—are kept closed.

These are the titles on the top row: *Out on the Pampas, With Lee in Virginia, By Right of Conquest, By England's Aid.* "Elizabeth Stewart, 1917," in Gran's loose script, is inscribed inside many. Below stands is an ancient row of children's adventure stories, bound fat in forest shades of fraying cloth.

Soft steps, and Aunt Helen appears at the door in her blue robe. She looks up at the bookshelf. "Hope you find something good in there—lots of them were your mother's."

"Thanks."

She sits at her desk, rummages through the top drawer.

"See if this is anything you'd want." She hands me a watch—stainless steel on a worn strap, the pigskin gone brown and glossy. I weigh it in my hand as I thank her and see that it's a Rolex.

"It's one of the first Oyster designs. Perpetual winding. You can wind it just by turning your wrist."

I turn the watch. A companionable *rrrrr* comes with each completed movement.

"It's made for forgetful people like myself," my aunt says. "Doesn't take much attention."

I thank her. Back in my room, I examine it with care.

. . .

The next day the fog burns off. It's clear, suddenly warm. The doors are open; the smell of cut lilies drifts down the hall.

Helen sweeps in, wearing her broad gardening hat, a basket of cut snapdragons over her arm.

"Oh, hullo! What a day! What do you say we row out for a picnic?"

Aunt Helen is followed everywhere by Guinness, her Belgian shepherd (something like a German shepherd, but with a longer snout, longer paws, soulful eyes). Guinness seems above the usual affectionate doggy behavior. He's well-behaved, quiet, a guardian of great dignity. There is also Fala, the white Lhasa—matted, full of burrs—who follows Guinness.

The cook has packed a lunch basket. Helen rows the Whaler down the cove to a small rock of an island, ten meters across at high tide. There, we eat ham-and-butter sandwiches and drink Coca-Cola from glass bottles.

"Food tastes better outside," says Helen, happier, more alert than these past weeks.

The dogs are excited; they run back and forth over the mass of rock and grey lichen. When the sandwich crusts are eaten and a dead crab wrested from Fala and thrown off into deep water, they go to sleep.

Aunt Helen asks about school and boys and we laugh a lot. Although small-boned and prone to jewels, Helen has a fine horsewoman laugh. We skip stones and flat shells across the water. Then, like the dogs, we nap on the warm rock.

We wake to find that we've forgotten the tide. The water has dropped; our little island is bigger, our rowboat marooned on the rocks.

The dogs are awake and excited, even the dignified

Guinness barking and running in circles as Helen and I strain to free the boat, the tops of our white Sperry sneakers and the bottoms of our jeans splashed dark and wet. Exhilarated, we row home.

Uncle Linc calls from his office in New York and asks for Felicity, who's out sailing.

"Maybe you can help," Linc says. "I hear that Helen isn't taking her medication. How does she seem?"

"Uhm—fine. We just rowed out for a picnic."

"I'd come up if I didn't think it would make it worse," Linc says.

"How do you mean?"

"You'd think that being at Stewart Cottage should help, but the doctors say that's not always so. . . ." He pauses. "Best not let your Gran know we've discussed this. She probably doesn't think I know. '*Not* the best person to consult on the subject,' she'd say. But I think that should classify me as an expert."

I still have no idea what he's talking about.

"So tell your cousin Felicity I called. . . ."

"O.K. I will. . . ."

"I was at Hazelden, you know," Linc says. "Not Silver Hill."

"Oh."

"Different treatments in those days. Shock."

The bathroom door is closed, but I hear the front door slam, Pearce's quick footsteps on the stairs.

"Meredith?" he calls.

"Yes?" I call back.

"Do you by any chance have hand lotion in there?"

I dry off and slip on a robe as Pearce's voice drifts in from the hallway.

"The Owens won the race using some boyfriend of the younger daughter—a ringer," he huffs. "Hired help at Northeast. Races Js. Certainly nothing to look at. Unfortunate skin and a nasty little ponytail."

Stepping over little lakes of chill, I open the door and pass him the bottle of Vaseline Intensive Care.

Pearce stands in a yellow foul-weather jacket, massaging the lotion into his palms.

"Felicity crewed for the Christopher brats again," he says. "At least *they* didn't win."

When Pearce was younger, he became bored with sailing and would use only the speedboat. Aunt Helen then sold the Hinckley, saying that Felicity was the only one who sailed it anyway, so why bother with upkeep. Now that Pearce likes sailing again, Helen rents him a boat, while Felicity continues with the Towles and the Christophers, crewing on their boats and eating at their tables.

"Is Felicity here for dinner?" I ask.

"I couldn't care less. Except, if you see her, tell her that, *as always,* she *does* need to let Stella know. Otherwise Mum's in a fix with the seating."

"O.K."

"Felicity's been rather inconsiderate about that," he sniffs, putting the bottle down on the ledge and leaning against the wall.

"Linc called." I pause. "He wanted to know about Aunt Helen's medication . . . ?"

"Good God, did Linc chew your ear off about that? She's taking it, I'm sure. It's just Felicity again—setting off false alarms. Everything's fine."

"Well. O.K."

"Good. Listen, I'll be in the kitchen. Want a planter's? We've got a pitcher made up."

I shake my head no. Pearce trots back downstairs, leaving a dark water mark on the wallpaper where he's been leaning.

—

There is a story from the summer Helen was six and my mother was four. That was 1945; everyone was happy about the war ending. The children's nanny was taking them from Long Island to Maine to see Gran and Grandaddy. "We're taking a train," their nanny told them, "then we're going to ride across the water on a ferry." The girls were quiet, well behaved on the train, happy with their picture books. Grandaddy's driver picked them up at the station and drove them to the ferry dock. As the attendant waved the car across the landing and onto the ferryboat, Helen looked around in astonishment. The nanny pointed out the car window and over the rail:

"Look, you can see the island in the distance. We'll be there in twenty minutes."

Helen cried tears and tears before she turned to the nanny accusingly and said, "You promised we'd ride on a fairy!"

In those days, expectations were high.

—

There's a *fwap-fwap* sound from high above—the yacht club flag rippling orange and white against a deep-blue sky.

Colin Bennett has been visiting all of August. Colin is Helen's first husband—Pearce and Felicity's father, in fact. Everyone gets on remarkably well.

Colin's visiting from England, where they still believe madness to be aristocratic. Today he wears a Greek fish-

erman's cap. Small children adore him and ask him to
blow the horn at races.

"Perfect day," says Colin.

"Mmm," says Felicity, smiling. She stretches her
legs—long and tan—in the sun.

Gordon Emerson joins us, bringing Felicity her grilled
cheese.

Hair short and shirt neatly tucked and pressed, Gordon
is a contrast to the boys at the other tables. "Oh—young
Gordon of the exceedingly straight nose," Colin dubbed
him last summer.

Most families come to the club for lunch. Orders are
placed at the grill window, the kitchen ladies marking slips
for each family. Behind them you can watch the burgers
sizzle, see the tubs of Crisco that line the shelves.

Colin leaves to check in on Helen, who's not feeling
well.

Gordon brings out two slices of blackberry pie. Felicity
wants hers with ice cream.

"This is *absolutely* a golfing sort of day," says Gordon.
"What do you think, Fel?"

"I'm racing with the Towles," she says.

Gordon gives me a lift back in his Subaru, pointing
out his favorite houses. Gordon's only seventeen, but with
a sense of history.

The houses are named for their original owners. New
people, however, come to the island. Fifteen years ago a
plastic surgeon named DeMassey bought the house on
Gilley Point. Gordon's great-great-grandfather Emerson
built the cottage in 1885—one of the first and grandest of
the summer colony. Dr. DeMassey remodeled it, put in a
glass-roofed porch, a sunken living room, a gym. Dr.
DeMassey invited the club members over for dinner, do-

nated money to the island fire squad, gave the new clay court at the tennis club. But the house was still known as Emerson Cottage; nothing the DeMasseys could do would change that. Last year Dr. DeMassey sold Emerson Cottage to a young Wall Street man with a blond personal secretary. These two are rarely seen.

Gordon wants to be an architect.

"What would be your first project?" I ask, making conversation.

"It couldn't be my first," says Gordon. "First, I'd have to make the money."

"Then what would you do?"

"Buy back Emerson Cottage, rip off that stinking glass porch." Gordon's face has an odd, set look. "Restore the hell out of it."

It's getting dark, and Helen's not down yet. Colin crouches in his chair, a new drink cradled in the same wet napkin as the last. The rain has stopped, but the mist still hangs, and suddenly it's a rare warm night on the island, the kind that makes your glass sweat.

Colin looks out to the dock. "There used to be a float at the end." He's drunk but speaks with the volume and precision of a man going deaf.

"Your uncle Harry kept seals out on that float. Pair of 'em. In a cage."

During the Second War, young Colin lived with the Fraser children, a refugee from the bombings. He stayed close with the family after the war, visiting every year.

Colin continues. "Was the summer before he started Groton. Forgotten how we got hold of the things, but Harry loved them. Would feed them in the late afternoon—mackerel, bait, that sort of thing. Very careful about their diet, read all sorts of books about it. Those seals were well kept. It was like Harry had some sort of mothering instinct. "We told Harry he should teach them tricks, circus tricks. You know, blow horns, walk on their front flippers, something like that. They only learned one. He'd hold a fish in his mouth, and they'd learn to scoot up and take it from him, sort of a seal kiss. I never tried it myself, thought they'd bite, but they never bit Harry. At the end of the summer Harry'd have them so that he didn't need the fish. Seals would stick their noses through the bars whenever they saw him walking down the dock. He'd bend down on his hands and knees and close his eyes and let them both kiss him. Seals would bark, and we'd all look down from the house. Sometimes he'd go into that cage, evenings like this, and roughhouse, roll around. Come back up wet and smelly and late for dinner." Colin pauses, squinting out to sea. "God, he loved those seals, Harry did. Kept them in a cage out on that float."

I am very afraid that Colin is going to cry. The serving girl comes out and does a quiet dip and smile in the doorway. It's time to go in for dinner.

Still no sign of Helen.

After dinner we retire to the living room and the coffee's passed. Pearce takes a red soda siphon and a box of seltzer cartridges from under the bar. Felicity excuses herself.

I've heard about whippets, but I don't realize that's what we're doing until after I've inhaled deeply and am holding my breath. I mean, I didn't know you used regular bar equipment, the kind even Gran has around. I'm about to let it out, to say "I don't feel anything," but I don't yet because I'm scared it will make my voice high and squeaky—the way with helium balloons—and I don't want to sound that way in front of Pearce. Then suddenly I start to laugh and have to put my head down between my knees and wait for the pressure to ease off. It's over very quickly, and I sit up, slightly weak.

"That must destroy brain cells," observes Colin from his chair.

Pearce stands in the center of the room, loading a fresh cartridge. His linen blazer is the color of crushed strawberries.

"Father, you lose as many with one drink."

"Yes, but a drink lasts longer."

Pearce raises the siphon to his lips and inhales. He lowers the container and stays straight and still as he reddens, holding his mouth closed, the corners turned up in a tight comic smile. He lifts his eyebrows and looks to me. Then, for effect, falls to the floor.

I wake late to a clear day, bright sun sneaking around closed curtains. I need liquids, I think, liquids and aspirin. I find aspirin in the bathroom and take it with two glasses of water. Tenderly, I put on my robe and circle my way down the staircase. Off the hall, the porch doors are open. The sun makes the sea shimmer blue, still and clear. Thinking to take my juice on the porch, I go into the kitchen, open the icebox, and reach for the glass pitcher. Just then Pearce, in bathing trunks and a polo, marches in from the pantry.

"Oops," Pearce says. "Careful. That's planter's for lunch. No OJ for late sleepers."

He trots through to the dining room, carrying place mats and knives. It bugs me how well my cousin looks on mornings when he should feel like hell.

"The Lowes are due at one. I'm making ribs." Joyfully, he trots back through to the pantry.

Amazing.

Felicity and I sit on the porch, out of the way of the lunch preparations. I have my back to a pillar, reading *Time* magazine. Felicity, cross-legged in a white T-shirt and cut-offs, combs her fingers through Guinness's coat, looking for ticks.

"Usually," Felicity says, "Mum and Pearce go to church if someone we know is doing a reading. Pearce thinks they ought to make an appearance."

"Is it me keeping them from it today? I would go if—"

"Good God no. Don't worry. Pearce simply *adores* making excuses for people after the service, saying they're not well. You can't stop him from that. You wouldn't believe how many people on this island think I'm sickly, which is a hoot because I've always been the healthiest person alive." Felicity pauses over Guinness's ruff, wrinkling her nose slightly. She tightens her grip and yanks at a tick. After examination, she tosses the little black ball over the lawn. "I should flush them, I know. But they die anyway when you pull them off like that. It tears off their heads." She strokes Guinness's muzzle. His tail swishes once against the floorboards, not ungrateful.

Pearce, strangely, likes to cook. Stewart Cottage, Pearce says, has the best kitchen in the world. It is large— three big rooms connected by wide open doorways, the walls cream with old gloss paint and the moldings and cabinets a shade called kitchen green, popular in the days when hostesses rarely saw their kitchens.

Billy and Amanda Lowe arrive at noon. They are old

friends and keep Pearce company as he prepares the marinade.

Billy wanders about the kitchen, picking up gadgets.

"I see your mother's raided Williams-Sonoma again. . . . Oh my God, what's this?" He picks up a threatening-looking object.

"Rolling mincer," answers Pearce.

"And this?"

"It's a timer. Just *look* at all this meat."

"Who's coming?" asks Amanda.

"*Us*. And Pops. Mum's not feeling well, and Felicity's driving a goddamn Christopher to the airport in Bangor. I'm thinking we should invite the Owens."

Amanda sighs. "If you must."

"Don't worry. It's last-minute. If they have any pride they'll say no."

The sun is hot on the porch. Mrs. Owen unfolds her napkin and looks about the table.

"Where's your mother?" she asks Pearce.

"Migraine."

The hired serving girl circles the table with platters of ribs and thin salty fries.

Mrs. Owen eats fries with a fork. Her white polo is sleeveless, baring the freckles on her tanned shoulders. She complains about a new family.

"I swear, if Travers disputes the race results *one* more time, I'm going to tack a bailer under his boat."

"*You* helped vote him in," says Pearce.

"Well, they'd bought Kirkwood Cottage—"

Pearce interrupts. "That's *just* the kind of thinking that gets us into this mess. If these awful new people buy one of the big houses, the members say, 'O.K., we'll let them in the club, take their dues, but we just won't speak to them and maybe they'll leave.' But it doesn't *work* that way. They don't seem to *notice* that we don't speak to them. They speak to each *other*. Then pretty soon they vote each other to the board, which in turn will vote to put up ugly bicycle racks and serve goddamned lobster Newburg at lunch. Case in point: the Swensons, who bought South Point—"

Mrs. Owen objects. "The Swensons are pretty nice. . . ."

Pearce looks astonished. "*Pretty* nice? Keep this in mind, Polly. You have young kids. Soon those kids will grow up. Who do you want them growing up with? Those 'pretty nice' Swenson kids? These are the kids your kids will first get drunk with. These are the kids your kids will first have sex with. Wouldn't you want them to be *more* than '*pretty nice*'?"

Mrs. Owen shrugs. "Best we can hope for, really."

A salad and cheese course follows, then Ben & Jerry's ice cream in neat little scoops on cut-glass dishes, molasses cookies at the side.

After lunch I'm with Pearce in the kitchen, standing over the meat grinder, helping him feed it strips from the ribs. "We can't waste it," Pearce says, and I think of looking into the icebox every morning and seeing the leftovers that Stella covered with plastic the night before, waiting to be thrown out three days later. But Pearce has plans for the meat; this afternoon he and Billy Lowe will take the speedboat to the mainland, where Pearce will buy Oriental rice wrappers. He's got a recipe for Szechuan pork dumplings for tonight's dinner.

At five o'clock I'm in the kitchen, heating the kettle for tea. Stella's back from her morning off and stands in a smock in the front pantry, putting away plates.

Pearce stamps in through the back door, clearly un-happy.

"They wouldn't sell me the *mussels!*"

"Who wouldn't?" I say.

"The goddamned restaurant."

Often, Pearce would speed Billy and maybe Colin to this particular dockside restaurant in Rockland, sit outside, and order pitchers of Long Island iced tea.

Pearce tells the story. The fish market was closed, so he and Billy sat down at this restaurant and asked for eight orders of mussels marinara to go.

"Certainly, sir."

"But please don't cook them," Pearce added.

"Excuse me?" said the waiter.

"Eight orders of mussels *to go;* please don't cook them."

"We don't do that, sir."

"But you'd sell them to me or any of these people *cooked?*" (Pearce acts his part loudly, gesturing around, as if to the restaurant.)

"Yes, sir. It is a hot dish."

"Well, can't you see I'm willing to *pay* the same *price.* I just want you *not* to cook them. I want only the *mussels;* I'm giving a *dinner.*"

"You just want eight orders of raw mussels, then?"

"*Exactly,*" Pearce said, with great finality.

"I'll speak with the chef."

For reasons unknown to him, Pearce didn't get the mussels.

Stella walks in from the pantry. She's overheard the trouble. "Aren't there mussels down by the pier?"

Pearce shrugs.

"Yes, there *are!*" Stella says, shaking a dishrag. "Perfectly *fine* mussels! Don't you remember from when you were little? When you'd go down to gather pearls—"

"You're thinking of Felicity," he mutters.

"No, it was both you children, sitting like little Indians, getting all fishy prying open shells to get at the pearls."

"Pearls, hah," Pearce says. "Puny things—weren't worth a dime."

Pearce leaves on an errand. Upstairs, Aunt Helen's door remains closed. Guinness, shut out, lies in front of her door, paws splayed like the gothic claws of a chair.

The phone rings. It's Linc.

"Is Felicity there?"

"No, she's not," I say.

"How's Helen feeling?"

"She's in her room. Did you want to speak with her?"

"No. Best not. Will you have Felicity call me when she gets back?"

"All right."

"Your aunt's a goddamn stubborn woman, you know."

I take a bucket down to the rocks. It's low tide, and I climb with Guinness behind me, taking slow shepherd-sized leaps. Down low between the rocks, in the wet rifts, I find mussels. They come off in large clumps, clinging to one another by gritty threads. I pry one apart, and indeed there are pearls. Many tiny pearls, pink and purple and gray. Wet and new and clinging together in my palm.

There on that cove it seemed that there were as many things right as were wrong but that nobody knew the difference or even where to begin.

Barbara, later that fall:

Your aunt was so spunky—feisty and funny. She'd ride faster than anyone else, ski down the ice hill at Broadhurst while your mother would sit with her nose in a book or sprawl on the floor cutting up magazines, making scrapbooks of horse show photos. Frankly, it got to where I wished I were Helen's guest and could run out and do something, not just sit there manning the jar of rubber cement while your mother cut Horse and Rider *to shreds.*

Both Helen and your mother were terrific riders— your mother took plenty of ribbons in dressage, Helen in jumping. The other girls would be mean and say that Helen always won because her father could buy the best jumpers, but this wasn't completely the case. She had good horses, but she also had nerve. There was so much life in her.

Then Helen turned eighteen—a season spent busily losing gloves and destroying as many pairs of satin shoes— then suddenly, poof! Married. Suddenly, there was this huge gulf between us, and I'd only see her in magazines: "Mrs. Colin Bennett, in the couple's London drawing room. Curtains by Colefax and Fowler."

Curtains indeed.

MOSS

Palo Alto, December 1983

My father is a collector, a man who loves art, order, ideas. He has an eye, putting objects together in a way one wouldn't have imagined—dry white sand dollars atop Californian pine boughs on the mantel at Christmastime, pre-Columbian rams bolstering framed anatomical drawings in the shelves in his study. In his office at the university, my father keeps a smooth, sun-bleached animal bone on his desk. He found this outside Palm Desert as a child and fancied it part of something rare and vanishing—a buffalo, a great cat. He now knows it to be the hind leg of a cow but keeps it anyway.

I'd unearthed the reel in the back hall closet while searching for wrapping paper. It was marked "Wedding: Heyton Hall, May 1963." I asked my father about it.

"Oh, Colin Bennett shot that. It's on sixteen millimeter, though. Not watchable."

I welcomed my father into the modern world and had the VHS tape back from Fotomat four days later.

The VCR is in Papa's study. He opens a bottle of Frascati and says to wait until the end of the evening news.

Heyton Hall, usually closed after April, was reopened for my mother's May wedding.

"Damn hot. Must have been close to a hundred," says Papa.

There's no sound on the video, but you can tell the day was still, no breeze. The pre-wedding lunch takes place on the edge of the back lawn, shaded by oaks. The camera pans in from far off, moves slowly toward the two picnic tables. I recognize Barbara Prewitt as she turns and grins for the camera.

The lunch is informal, the women in Bermuda shorts, sleeveless shirts. There are no more than twenty guests, the wedding kept small because of Harry's death. The heat affects the group; they lounge—loose in the joints, content, immobile.

The camera pans down the table. There's my father, smiling huge at the camera. He looks handsome, neat, clean shaven in a crisp, short-sleeved oxford. Beside him is my mother.

My mother's beauty does not surprise me. I have seen Gran's pictures of her at this age, each one remarkable. But Gran's photos are in black and white, this film is color. As the camera pulls close on my mother's face, she's smiling serenely, not shying away as I would come to expect.

Her skin is flawless, translucent, cheeks lightly flushed at the apple. It is a radiant, beautiful face, purely constructed and of absolute health.

"She looks great," I say to my father.

"She always did," he answers, and I'm not sure which he means: *Yes, she did then,* or *she did always.* I don't ask.

My mother's shoulders are bare under the narrow straps of a stiff cotton bathing suit, the kind with a skirt, the kind she'd never wear again. She has a calm, sleepy smile that I'd seen only rarely—when she smoked a joint or watched the dogs chase sticks. Loosely, she holds a small wineglass and gazes at the camera, head cocked to one side.

"Dubonnet," says Papa. "Always had a hard time getting her to take a drink, but she could get so sweet after half a glass of Dubonnet."

My mother continues to gaze sleepily, uncharacteristically, until the camera cuts.

In a far shot, I pick out Linc by his walk—hands in his pockets, stiff-kneed, weight swaying sturdily from one leg to the other, the walk of an older, heavier man. The camera comes in closer as he approaches the picnic table. Linc wears long rumpled khakis, even in the heat. His short-sleeved madras shirt, untucked, clings to him.

Helen sits, back straight, in a cool sleeveless shift, her hair sprayed and lifted into a smooth mass, no bits or pins falling. The camera pulls back, and we see that she has a small pug in her lap. This is the kind of little dog not generally seen at Heyton Hall and belongs perhaps to a guest. Helen holds a cup up to the pug as it laps water. My mother, used to bigger, nobler dogs, looks on, expressionless.

The film cuts away, then we see Gran, in a mannish

straw hat, walking over to grip my mother's shoulder. Quickly, quickly, she pulls her up and, still holding her shoulder, propels her toward the house. Somehow the pace has gone to Keystone Cops, as if someone has sped up the film. Papa laughs, turns slightly red.

"Your mother months later told me that was for the talk on how to manage your husband. She was mortified. 'I'd even rather it had been about sex,' she said."

On-screen, the scene has changed. It must be later—the light's going. Briefly, we see three flutists, all in black, setting up. Then the guests arrive, the same twenty or so from lunch, seated in two rows of benches under a green oak allée, the marsh beyond. The service itself is not filmed, so the next thing we see is the bride's back as, holding her arm, my father leads her away.

They walk under colonnades of live oak, each burled trunk rising dark and thick, casting intricate shadows on the carpet of ryegrass. The bride holds her skirt as she walks, a pretty gesture. All you can see of her are her elbows beneath the cap sleeves of the dress, the rest hidden by the satin train of the gown, the fall of her veil. Her new husband bends down as they walk and he says something to her.

My father has been watching intently. "I told her it was like being in church," he says, voicing exactly what I was thinking about the vaulted boughs, the cast of light. "She smiled when I said that, but I think she was blind to all of it."

"If I had Heyton Hall I'd never leave it," I say, then think to add, "She looks happy, though."

"If she looked happy here, it's because she was getting away."

"I'm sure that's not the only reason."

"It's all right if it is," Papa says, stroking his beard

with two fingers. "A strange but beautiful woman, your mother."

And then there is the reception. Daylight's failing, so all we have are two shots: one of Gilbert in his white jacket, holding a tray of champagne glasses glowing gold, then one of Linc lighting Gran's cigarette.

——

A photo from Gran's album:

My mother sits on the top step of the front porch at Heyton Hall, squinting into the sun. She's about thirteen, wearing jodhpurs she'll grow into, a flannel check shirt. Her tall boots are close to the camera and look huge. Bobo, the spaniel, rests his spotted muzzle across her lap, long curly ears dangling down, dirty paws on her britches.

And the thing is, she looks perfectly happy.

——

The tape is off; Papa's deep into the wine.

"So there we were, married. When we set up our apartment near campus we realized she could barely boil water. So I did the cooking, which it turned out I was pretty good at, but it bothered the hell out of her. Whenever I'd put a plate in front of her, or carry a roast out of the kitchen, she'd moan about being a failure as a wife.

"That summer we went to Paris for a honeymoon. Seemed like the thing to do.

"At school we'd eaten in coffee shops—your mother liked coffee shops—but they didn't seem to have coffee shops around the Ritz in Paris. I'd want to go out to a good restaurant; she wanted room service. This went on for three nights. 'Honey,' I'd say, 'if you're tired, we'll just eat downstairs.' 'No!' she'd answer. We talked, and it turned out it wasn't restaurants that bothered her—it was the headwaiters. They terrified her—so intimidating. As a girl she'd always eaten at home. Restaurants were for people without kitchen staff." Papa pauses, then continues.

"You know, my fondest memory of your mother is her in a blue cotton nightgown, sitting cross-legged on the bed at the Ritz, gnawing on a steak bone. You could see the lights of Paris through the window behind her, but there she was, cross-legged on the bed, gnawing on this bone."

HARVESTS

Whenever Mama ran away from Papa, she'd try to make it look noble.

The first time was in 1970, to Mississippi, to teach in the Head Start program. It was a place with few trees—the soil was too poor to grow anything but peanuts and patchy weeds. My mother and I lived for several months in a muddy trailer near the schoolhouse, the only white people for miles.

Down the road, Sadie, who had her grandchildren living with her, would feed me graham crackers and Coca-Cola. I think my first memory may have been of sitting in her kitchen at a red-and-white oilcloth-covered table and overhearing Sadie say, "Lord, it's a crime how she makes that child live that way."

Papa tracked us down through the Fraser Foundation,

which funded Head Start. He agreed to a lot to get her back: that they'd change things together, would call themselves "partners," since by then Mama had gotten it into her head that marriage was slavery.

And for a while Papa went along with the commune idea—amused, patient.

Oregon. Mama's twenty acres included the house and barn, two fields, an orchard, and a clear brown creek rimmed with skunkweed. That winter of '72 it was just Mama, Papa, and me in the farmhouse, then with the spring came Jan and Mike, Olivia and John.

When John and Olivia split up, Olivia and her children stayed on with us in the house, while John built a tepee down by the creek. Soon John had a new woman, and then the cabin people came. Stan and Mimi built their cabin using wooden pegs instead of nails, then, with John's help, constructed a canvas and stone sauna hut. The night the hut was completed, I remember wearing my one-piece bathing suit while the adults sat circled naked around the fire and glowing rocks. I couldn't stand the temperature, the low walls, the nakedness, so I slunk outside. Later I watched as the adults ran whooping from the hut to wade out into the shallow creek, where they would splash their bodies, already wet.

The next day Olivia's children and I gathered the blackened chars from the fire pit and painted char stripes on our noses and cheeks to play Indians. The adults saw us do this and joined in, blackening their whole faces and then painting their bodies, passing the chars over each other's shoulders and chests, arms and legs, letting go with low war cries while, embarrassed, we children washed our faces by the plank bridge.

• • •

Papa left the spring of '73, after Mama and the others painted the mural. I woke early one morning to find one whole wall of the kitchen painted as the Garden of Eden: a Day-Glo orchard with a huge round sun, fat birds and animals. In the center stood Adam and Eve, pink and life-sized. The paint was still sticky, and someone had arranged clusters of chicken feathers where pubic hair would be.

I was eating a brownie when my mother came in, wrapped in a ragged blanket.

"Oh—don't eat that," she said. "Those are the grown-ups' funny kind. . . ."

Mail would arrive from back east. The rusty red-flagged RFD mailbox was the focus of my day. I loved bringing in the letters; I'd recognize the ones from Gran or Aunt Helen—pale smoke-blue envelopes that crackled from their thin tissue lining.

Cardboard boxes holding the Social Register arrived periodically; Mama would toss them out unwrapped. I rescued one of the black and orange volumes from the trash heap, liking its thickness, its weight. If Mama had looked inside, she would have seen that she was still listed and cross-listed, her maiden name under "Dilatory Domiciles" and her address reading "Mrs. Charles W. Scott (Sarah Fraser)—*The Farm*, Monroe, Oregon." I suppose it was Helen who maintained the listing, as *The Farm* was italicized in that wistful way I would later recognize as denoting a vacation cottage or country house.

At Christmas Mama would receive cards from girls she'd known at Radcliffe and open them dutifully. They'd almost always feature a photo: one or two children with flossy just-brushed hair, white piqué collars, and a rabbit or kitten on the garden bench. Or they'd show a larger family lined up on skis—matching goggles, mittens and new plastic boots, bright on the snow.

"Isn't it strange that CeeCee would track me down out here," Mama would say. But I knew, even then, that it wasn't strange at all. Even on the farm, it was as hard for Mama to hide as if she were an elephant behind a birch tree.

Mama wanted to grow things, thought that that would make life pure. But she soon discovered that plants die, that people cheat and steal. She found that in Oregon it rains and rains. We didn't really grow crops, but there was the apple orchard and one field of wheat. The first year, Mama and the others harvested and threshed the wheat by hand; a three-day project, drinking wine. Mama played at grinding the wheat with a mortar and pestle, just a few batches. Then she baked bread, which we ate with Cheez Wiz because that's all they sold at the convenience store down the road.

That fall the men made a cider press and the rest of us gathered fallen apples. We all rode in a truck to a crafts fair in the woods outside Portland, where we set up a stand and pressed the juice into small paper cups for which we charged twenty-five cents apiece.

Since there were about twenty of us and only one press, Mama and I were free to walk around to look at the handmade puppets, papier-mâché dragons, wooden masks. "Everyone's selling something," she said, without emotion.

With the third winter coming, Mama had mixed feelings about the farm. She started talking about going to Canada, maybe getting a job teaching school. We started to drive the truck, but it died just past Junction City. We left it there, hitched into Eugene, where she said we could catch a train. She tried to get me to look forward to the trip; talked about Christmas in Canada, hot chestnuts and snow. Now I see that she was running away.

But that didn't matter, because she hadn't checked the train schedule. By the time we'd walked around Eugene, she'd rented a two-bedroom apartment. There, I remember reading comics and eating cream of mushroom soup while it rained outside.

In a few weeks we moved back to the farm. Mama started to weld, with large tools and blue flame, in the lean-to behind the barn. She would experiment with tin from the roof of the fallen down toolshed, shaping small bits, the grey edges melted smooth and swirled with the color of fire.

She gave that up when the weather got colder. There was no room in the house for her equipment, because by then she had given away all the rooms except our two in the attic.

I liked the farm, but then again, I had a pony.

I rode my pony to school. Mama and the two bigger dogs—Tulip and Legs—would walk beside me. But as I got older I was embarrassed; the other kids arrived by bus or in trucks. I started walking to the nearest spot on the school bus route.

I was shy with the other children but liked my teacher. There were only four classrooms for the eight grades— Miss Robertson taught the first and second. She wore tidy blouses with point collars, short skirts, pink lipstick. One day I had to take home a permission slip for Mama to sign. My class was going on a field trip to the airport in Eugene.

My mother wrote this on the slip: "My daughter has been in numerous airports and is wholly familiar with them. Please excuse her from the trip."

Mama eventually took me out of school, saying I was needed at home for the harvest. They let parents do that in Oregon.

At about that same time she said I couldn't visit my one school friend, Laurie, who had spiral curls like Cindy Brady, bright-yellow jeans with coordinated tees, and a mother who pierced ears and made Rice Krispies treats while we watched *Hee Haw*.

Mama said I'd spend my time with her. She'd take me with her across the creek to gather mushrooms in the woods. Then, with our baskets and the two dogs, we'd walk up the next hill and cross the paved road to the Larkins'.

The Larkins were an old couple who lived in a square blue house behind an aluminum gate. Mama would sit at Mrs. Larkin's dining room table and they'd sort through the mushrooms. Mrs. Larkin would tell Mama which ones were good and which were poison.

Like Sadie before her, Mrs. Larkin would fix me a plate. There were salty Bacon-O crackers from a box, which I didn't get at home, and a glass of milk, which I didn't get, either. Mrs. Larkin and Mama would begin sorting mushrooms, while after my snack, I'd play quietly in the living room.

But, as I said, those walks with my mother began in the woods, the dark moist places where mushrooms grew. We'd find them growing at tree trunks and wet ground, the best ones yellow and brown, large and tattered.

Now when I think of these forest trips—the black pungent bark, the floor of rotting leaves—I get a shiver. But I don't shiver from remembering the cold or damp; nor was I scared. The forest itself felt safe; I did not mind the leaf-living creepies, the crawlies, the brown rolling centipedes.

No, what makes me shiver is the image of my mother. I am not proud of that. Walking beside her, I was all too conscious of the straggled, dulled hair, the leathered exposed skin, the damage of sun and wind. I was acutely aware of the callused patches on her cheeks, the dry cracked sores on her lips. I could not look at her face when she spoke to me.

I did not know my mother when she was perfect. I was a baby then. But as I grew, I knew one thing. I kept very quiet about it, because I knew to think it was wrong. What I thought was that this was *not* my mother. What I thought was that I hated this mushroom gatherer, and what had she done with my mother?

One early morning, September '76, the dogs were shot running sheep. Mama shut herself in her room and cried for what seemed days. I ate Cheez Wiz on apples, because that's all there was. At the end of that week we went back to my father.

She died two years later, after leaving again. This time I'd stayed with my father. I held Papa as he cried but did not ask for the truth. There seemed nothing brutal about the expected.

For my next birthday, Aunt Helen sent a present. A white boxed cardigan sweater and a thin book with a yellow jacket called *What to Do, When and Why*. It was an etiquette book written by two Washington ladies. Inside, precise pen-and-ink drawings showed girls with heart-shaped faces, even hairlines, and wide-sashed dresses making introductions, rising gracefully from chairs, and penning thank-you notes at well-appointed desks. I loved this book; still have it, in fact.

But soon I'd be at Heyton Hall, uncertain of when to stand, when to sit.

THE
WISHBONE

**Heyton Hall, South Carolina,
Thanksgiving 1984**

This is how I learned to shoot. Pearce
and Lamont had me out on the traps, shooting clay.
"Pull," they taught me to call, showing me how to raise
the rifle to my shoulder and steady myself against the hard
kick of wood.

I got the very first disk, shattering it into satisfying
bits. But as I tried to remember how I'd done it, the game
got harder. Lamont would launch the disks at the same
angle as before; they'd spin over the marsh, hover, then
sail down, untouched.

My arm was aching. "One more," I said. Pearce stood
alongside with his gun, waiting his turn.

The disk whistled as I pulled and shot. A crow was passing at the time; the bird fell, the disk sailed on.

"Oh, God . . . I'm sorry," I said.

"Woo! Meredith—not to be bothered with these *clay* things!" cried Pearce.

"Got you a crow. . . . That's a sign of somethin'," said Lamont.

"A sign for her never to call her shot in billiards," said Pearce. He turned to Lamont. "Hey, shouldn't we blood her or something?"

The banister curves down the stairway to the hall and dining room, the steps carpeted in doe-colored runner and scattered with squares of morning light.

From downstairs I hear voices, the kitchen door swinging open, then closed. Two girls in white uniform pass, loads of towels under their arms, a water pitcher held precariously.

I run into Pearce at the base of the stairs. "Wow," he says. "You should get up earlier—you miss everything."

"What's happened?"

"Felicity's left."

Last night before dinner Pearce led me halfway down the stairs.

"*Shh!*" he said. Voices rose from the gun room.

Felicity was saying that she'd spend Christmas with her father in England—"certainly not tramping around some goddamn ring like a braided pony."

"The invitations are out, our friends are coming, it's paid for. . . ." Helen's voice carried faintly. "You can't simply *drop out*."

"Mother, kindly remember that I never dropped *in* to start with."

"We discussed this *ages* ago. . . ."

"And I said no then, and I'm saying no now."

"It's only a few days, just some—"

"Pointless teas and thank-you notes. No, thanks."

"Really, if only you—"

"Mother, I went to Madeira. Wasn't that enough?"

Helen began to tire. "Your name is on the invitation. You can't simply—"

"Bull." Short and curt.

So that was last night.

"So it's settled?" I ask.

Pearce shrugs. "The FedEx man just came by with Felicity's air tickets to London. She's definitely spending Christmas with Papa."

"Oh."

"Leaving December *twentieth*. I think Mum's finally gotten it into her head that old Sourpuss really won't attend."

"But aren't the invitations out?"

"They're certainly printed. Not that Felicity gives a hoot. It's just one of those big group things anyway, more a brawl than a ball. Listen, I'd say to screw it too. But now Mum's got smoke coming out her ears, muttering it's all planned."

"She must be disappointed."

"I'll say. Raises my stock anyway. Well—breakfast at your own risk. Ciao." Pearce bounds up the stairs.

Breakfast is English style, meaning people come when they like; the women when they rise, the men after a shoot. All except for Gran, who has a tray brought to her room, plates under silver warmers.

Sun streams across polished mahogany and glazed

quail-print mats. A lead-crystal and silver honey pot in the shape of a bumblebee catches the light.

Helen sits over tea and toast crumbs, tapping her foot. We exchange "Good mornings."

Gilbert enters, black tie square at the bottom, clipped to his shirt with a gold bar.

"Good mornin', Miss Meredith. What would you like for breakfast?"

It's gotten so that I can say "The usual, please," meaning one egg poached, toast, and bacon.

Gilbert pours my tea. I add honey from the bee-shaped server.

Helen lets out a small sigh and turns her eyes to me.

"How old will you be next Christmas, dear?"

"Eighteen."

"Hmm."

After breakfast I stop by Gran's room to say good morning. She sits up in a bed jacket, grey hair pulled back neatly, reading a fat political memoir through black-framed glasses while the fire crackles and blazes. I sit in the chair closest to the fire, feel the heat against my leg.

I tell Gran about Helen's plan.

"Do you think it's all right if I come out next year?" I ask. "The thing is, I'll be eighteen, but I won't be in college yet."

"I wouldn't know about these things, dear, but I'm quite certain there are people who would."

"Aunt Helen says it will be fine, and she's on the committee and all."

Gran narrows her eyes. "Do you *want* to do this?"

I tell her that I do indeed.

Gran shrugs. "Then do."

• • •

It's Gran, Helen, Linc, Pearce, and myself for Thanksgiving lunch. Slices of turkey surround rows of roast dove on Gilbert's platter; a dish of stuffing follows.

"So I hear I've been spared deb duty for another year," says Pearce to no one in particular.

Linc looks around the table. It's just occurred to him. "Where's Felicity?"

Helen makes a face, doesn't answer.

Pearce holds out the tiny wishbone from his dove. "Pull and make a wish," he tells me.

After lunch I hang around the kitchen. Chessy is wrapping cold dinner plates in plastic—she and the staff have the evening off to spend with their families.

Bonnie, Linc's hound, barks at the back door, wanting to be let in. Chessy opens the door and puts some cut-up turkey into a bowl, which she places on the floor.

"You remember my Buttercup?" Chessy says. Chessy misses her poodle. "Your uncle Linc gave me that dog. Buttercup lived seventeen years. My daughter, she say, 'Mama, why don't you get another dog?' but Buttercup, he was my dog."

"Is your daughter here for the holiday?" I ask, perched on a stool.

"Oh, yes, her and my little grandson."

"Where are they usually?"

"Raleigh," Chessy says. "She's a stenographer up there, works in the courthouse. Not much to do round here for her, not much." She slides the wrapped plates into the refrigerator.

Pearce goes off somewhere that evening, saying, "I don't eat leftovers." I stay up late, reading. At ten

77

past midnight I hear the car, the gravel crunch on the driveway.

Pearce walks into the living room, spots me, and says, "Hello. You're up late." He sees the plate and fork on the end table. "Where'd you get the pie?"

"The kitchen."

"That's off-limits at night."

"It is?"

"That mincemeat from lunch?"

"Uh-huh."

The light from the stove hood is left on. The faint hum of refrigerators makes it all seem more quiet.

"I don't think I've snuck in here since I was little," Pearce says.

"You're joking."

Pearce wanders, opening cabinets.

There are four refrigerators. The one in the front pantry is for the bar: pitchers of juice, bottles of seltzer, slices of lemon. The one in back holds large pieces of meat, half gallons of milk. In the main kitchen there are two, which contain tubs of lard with plastic lids held tight by suction, pie dishes under Saran Wrap, leftovers in plastic bowls, loaves of Roman Meal bread.

The cabinets are packed full with orderly rows of large-count boxes: one hundred Lipton tea bags, five-hundred-count Dixie Crystals, two-hundred-fifty-count Diamond toothpicks, "round." Then there are at least forty cans of Campbell's beef broth, six boxes of Bisquick, a couple of cartons of Wheat Thins, a can of Chessy's strawberry Slim-Fast.

The counters are bare, except by the stove, where there's a tub of butter with a caulking knife stuck into it.

"Shouldn't the butter be refrigerated?" I ask Pearce.

"I shouldn't think so. Probably go through three pounds a day. That's why Chessy looks the way she does." He bends his knees and leans into the freezer, searching for ice cream.

Pearce sits on the table by the window with his slice of pie, inspecting the pile of magazines: *Star, Jet,* the Spiegel catalog. "So that's how they spend their time," he says. "No wonder the water pitchers don't get filled!"

I'm perched with my plate against the counter.

"Actually, they're pretty busy all day. You wouldn't believe how many loads of laundry."

"Oh, I'm sure I wouldn't." Pearce slices a bit of pie with his fork, careful to include an equal amount of ice cream on top. "By the way, I've meant to mention that. You're getting a little old to be hanging around the kitchen."

"I like kitchens."

Pearce takes another bite, swallows. "It's just that it's impolite to the staff."

"How do you mean?"

"Well, Chessy and Gilbert wouldn't tell you because it would be rude, but they have their jobs and you have yours."

"My job?" I ask. "What's that?"

This is perhaps the first time I've seen Pearce flustered. "Well . . . sort of like . . . being a Fraser."

I look back at him. "But I'm not, really."

"Don't be silly. Of course you are. And I'm sure you'll do a bang-up job, once you get the hang of it."

There's a photo in Papa's collection, one from Mississippi: *The boy and I are both maybe three years old, eating*

79

Popsicles. We're standing together in front of a red and white Coca-Cola cooler—big, like a refrigerator on its side. You can see the grey concrete wall of the store behind it, you can tell it's dusty hot.

My friend is black, dark black, in a red checked shirt and khaki shorts, both fresher than my overalls. I don't remember his name, but he was one of Sadie's grandchildren.

The concrete-block store sold gas and groceries. There was a wire carousel of toys packaged in cellophane: guns, red balls on paddles, plastic Miss America crowns. In the back, a glass-doored refrigerator (the glass fogged, rivulets of water running down) held tubs of Brunswick stew, water puddling on plastic lids. There was also a jar of pickled pigs' feet, which I'd stare at. The hooves were packed in pink liquid, but where the flesh and bone pressed against the glass, I could see that the meat was dead white.

I also remember red jawbreakers at the register, a full mason jar. And a rack of peanut butter crackers, packed in plastic. I begged my mother for these. These, the toys, and the crown. I remember she'd say we didn't have the money. I doubt I believed her then. I suppose that's why I remember it now.

ONE YEAR
LATER

New York, November 1985

The fitting room carpet is industrial grey. In the corner stands a rack of suspiciously beaded evening dresses. I stand in front of a long mirror, my arms crossed, hands splayed against the gaping bodice.

Helen perches on a gilt chair, saying, "You're an angel, Philippe, doing this on a Saturday."

Mr. Robertson kneels, with a mouthful of pins, plotting my hem. "Give ze young lady what she wants, no?"

The dress is an ivory strapless satin sheath with a slight bustle, trimmed in silk roses. "Ivory, not dead white," said Aunt Helen. "White does nothing for skin like ours."

I'd assumed that Helen would recreate her own coming-out dress, but she is not sentimental that way.

When I asked her if she'd kept her dress, she'd shaken her head and looked at me as if I'd asked something odd. It made me think of Colin, something he'd said: "Helen used things up."

Mr. Robertson, still pinning, asks me to take a quarter turn.

From her chair, Helen asks, "Meredith, are you sure you can't manage a higher heel?"

DEBUT

"Are you having a good time? Do you like your table?" Aunt Helen adjusts her pearls, sliding the clasp to the back of her neck.

"Oh, a wonderful time."

"Pearce and you looked nice, dancing."

"He's a good dancer."

We're in the ladies' room of the Waldorf, in front of the long mirror—gilt, with movie star lights, glass dishes of powder and bobby pins beneath. Aunt Helen herded me in to rearrange the bow on the back of my dress. "It looks crooked; it's bothering me," she'd said after the salad course.

I'm nervous; the presentation is soon. My father has

stayed out west, pointing out that none of this was his idea. "This is Helen's show," he said. (She said, "I wish your father could have come. . . . Not that it's not perfectly all right having Linc present you, but heaven knows he's apt to trip.")

Now Aunt Helen reapplies lipstick, camellia pink. She looks young tonight, her skin English pale and moist, the fine lines puffed up with cream. Her dress is a narrow, sleeveless, silver grey Givenchy. At her neck she wears a short row of pearls, large as grapes. Their size makes her limbs look even smaller, more fragile.

Helen smooths her lipstick with a tiny gold brush. "This color would be good on you, no?"

When she says this I'm looking in the mirror and wondering if everyone's right—if that's me in twenty-five years.

"Thanks," I say, and take the tube.

Standing with the fathers, Linc shuffles. Down the line some of the men look proud, some too warm, some uncomfortable in tails. Several drink Scotch, but Linc doesn't. He looks stiff and nervous, like most of the girls (those not the group leaning against the back wall, smoking cigarettes).

Conversation with the others made me nervous. Aunt Helen had told me the dress-fitting weekend—just seeming to *mention*, in an oh-by-the-way fashion—that if anyone should ask, I was to say that I was at Westminster for a "postgraduate year."

"But I thought you said my age was O.K.," I'd protested.

"Yes, it's fine. But I told the committee that you were taking an extra year to prepare for college, to adjust from those West Coast schools. They quite understood."

So when girls asked where I went to school, I said simply "Westminster" and they'd nod, thinking perhaps that it was an obscure little college and politely dropping the subject.

Helen comes to check on us in line. "Those other girls are slouching," she says. "Don't you two slouch."

The presentation is painless, no one trips, the escorts cut in on the fathers, the floor committee on the escorts. With more dancing, things get looser and the girls drink more and more and I can't find Pearce.

"You're a lovely dancer," says the red-haired boy in the middle of a Cole Porter medley. He's wearing a red sash, marking him as part of the floor committee, who have to say nice things.

"Thank you," I say, thinking how the sashes make them look like mock dignitaries, pretend princes.

"Lovely girl too. But if I may say so, you're being rather badly escorted."

"He's my cousin."

"Ah, good."

The boy gives me more charming compliments. From some committee handbook, I'm sure, but I'm grateful.

———

On Helen's bedside table there is a photo, silver-framed, her June debut date engraved at the bottom. In the photo she's dancing with Grandfather. She wears layer upon layer of white organza, a cloud, a pillow of a dress. The buttercup sleeve exposes the sharp curve of her arm, cut by white kid. Grandaddy's smiling, sleek as a cat. His hand's high on Helen's back as he pushes her around the dance floor.

In the background, Gran's sitting at a table with two women of her age and position. All three wear their hair in the marcel waves of the previous generation. Dark dresses cover their shoulders, and heavy brooches sit centered below the breastbone. Gran has her arms folded, a cigarette in one hand, the other women rest their elbows on the table beside the demitasse. It's late, clearly.

———

"Your eyes ought to be registered as lethal weapons." The president of the Beta house at Tulane guides me backward, his lead tight, elbows close to his sides, voice like honey. His feet are quick and practiced; he squares off in neat boxes, small like the flat grosgrain bows of his slippers. Flat gold studs descend his shirtfront, a white-on-white latticework of small woven diamonds. It's a night of glittering objects.

Crimson velvet ribbons the ballroom columns; garlands of holly snake toward the ceiling. The crimson matches the favor for each deb on her table's centerpiece: a velveteen and lace ornament, a souvenir, something to hang at eye level on her Christmas tree through many winters and marriages, there to remind her of so many steps in so short a time that she got dizzy and had to sit down. Or perhaps there was one perfect dance toward the end of the evening, when she was winded and her hem trod on, grey shoeprints on white, and she felt relief because she didn't have to worry anymore.

The band's playing "You're the Top."

" 'You're the Tower of Pisa,' " the Tulane boy sings at a hush. " 'You're the top, you're the Mona Lisa . . .' "

"Can we sit this one out?" I ask.

"Well, hell yes, honey."

Pearce hasn't crossed my vision for hours. He has a room upstairs at the hotel, so I don't think he's left.

I see Aunt Helen sitting with an old man, a friend of Gran's. She's looking pained and jittery, but beautiful.

"Jed," I say, his palm at my back, guiding me off the dance floor.

"Yeh, honey . . . ?"

"Would you be an angel—" I look down, pausing a bit on the word, awkward with it. It is Helen's word, not mine. But then I look up and see that the man's not laughing. Rather his eyes are welling with interest.

"Would you be an angel and ask my aunt to dance?"

"Sure, Darlin'. Whatever you say." He seats me. "But I'll be back."

I sit, kick my shoes off under the table, look around. Still no sign of him.

—

Helen's dance was at Broadhurst—early June, under a tent. Barbara told me how beautiful Helen looked, that pillow of a dress. The only thing to mar the evening for Helen was that Harry couldn't come back from London. He sent the news by telegram so that he couldn't be reached with questions. He'd often disappear that way, pretending he didn't think he'd be missed. But of course, all anyone heard that evening was "Where's Harry?"

FIREWORKS

We drive behind a rusted yellow bus, the back of which reads, in black block letters: FOLLOW ME TO CHURCH.

We're driving east toward Hilton Head. Late afternoon light cuts through the trees and casts patterns on the hood of the red Morgan. This is Pearce's new car. He's sold the Jag ("now that everyone and their dentist has one").

We pass low tin-roofed churches needing paint, cement-block groceries fronted with gas pumps. Passing open land, we can see the grey wispy smoke of brush burning.

Down a dusty driveway I see signs stenciled in red on

white board: "Peaches," "Tomatoes," "Vidalia Onions." I ask Pearce if these aren't out of season—are the signs up all year? He shrugs.

Further down the road we begin to see billboards for golf courses, time shares, mill outlets, Hardees.

"Not long now," says Pearce.

Pearce gives the guard at the Sea Pines gatehouse a name I've never heard. "Grandparents of a girl I used to know," he says when I ask.

We follow the paved road to the end of the island and park the car in an empty drive. The tree trunks on the beach path are twisted with vines grown grey and hard. The air has the smoky sweetness of old wood, the last rain.

On the beach, we take our shoes off to walk, leaving them by a smooth grey log. The fine sand is packed hard; there are wide views up and down the empty beach. Distantly, we can see the harbor lights of Beaufort. A slight cool breeze rustles the sea oats; the light is fading blue.

The houses are set back from the beach, a polite distance.

"You see," says Pearce, "Sea Pines isn't a *bad* place, but the problem is it *started* the trend. . . ."

"What trend?"

"Dividing land into lots. For golfing people."

"Like that place on Daufuskie?"

"Yes. A business place. Golfers. Northerners with what they think is money."

"We're Northerners," I say.

"Not really," says Pearce.

"Well, we're not Southern, either."

"Did I say we were Southern?"

"No, though I guess that I've always liked the idea."

"Of being Southern?"

"Yes."

"Where'd you get a weird idea like that?"

"I don't know. Maybe from the time I was little. When my mother and I visited at Easter."

"Which Easter?"

"Your mother's wedding."

"Oh, right." He kicks at the sand.

Silence.

"So where *are* we from?" I ask.

"We're from Chicago."

"I've never been to Chicago."

Pearce shrugs.

Something occurs to me. "And couldn't you and Felicity just as easily be English?"

"Well, we are, sort of," he says. "But these things pass down the maternal line."

"Really?"

"Yes."

"All right, then. Grandaddy was born in Chicago, but Gran was born in Hartford. Wouldn't that mean that our mothers would be from Hartford?"

"No. Absolutely not." Pearce shakes his head violently.

"Well, that's good. So I guess you mean your rules are flexible."

"I suppose. . . ." He's confused.

"Good. Does that mean I get to be Southern?"

"Now, *why* would you want to be Southern?"

"Oh . . . I don't know. All those things lost . . . The wisteria . . ."

"Hysteria?"

"*Wisteria*. Those purple flowers. The ones that hang like grapes."

"We don't have purple flowers at Heyton Hall."

"Yes we do. On the wire-link fence by the tennis courts."

"Oh, those weeds . . ."

"Yes."

"You like those weeds?"

"Yes."

"Hmm."

We walk in silence for a bit. "So why do you choose Chicago?" I ask.

"I didn't *choose* Chicago," he says.

"You just said you did."

"No I *didn't,* Meredith. You're confused."

"You *did.*"

We walk on a bit farther.

I draw lines through the hard sand with my toe as we sit on a beached log of soft driftwood. We watch the waves, their slight foam as they crest, roll, hit the beach. Farther out, the ocean is calm.

"So who gets Heyton Hall when Gran dies?" I ask.

"Why? Do you want it?" Pearce inspects an urchin shell, dispassionately.

"Well . . . I'm just curious."

"I understand it's to be sold. It's a hard place to run. Prohibitively expensive just to keep to shoot a few weeks out of the year. The best that can happen is if Gran sells it to someone rich enough not to subdivide. That's what's happened to other places down here."

"Won't you be sad to see it go?"

"Yes, but like I said, it's very expensive to keep up." Pearce looks back at me. "You don't shoot. Why would you want it?"

"Couldn't someone just live there?" It sounds like a question, though I don't mean it to be.

"Why would you want to live there?"

"It's the prettiest place I know." I am somehow embarrassed when I say this. I used to imagine myself, older, sitting on the porch in a long print cotton dress with the marsh far behind me. There would be a pitcher of iced tea on the table and a cutting basket of camellias at my feet. I wonder why I am ashamed of this.

"Well," Pearce says, "the best thing for the place is if Gran finds a buyer who can afford to keep it up. Not developers, not the state. It'll take a miracle."

"The New York Park Service ruined Broadhurst, didn't it?"

"*Gran* ruined Broadhurst."

"By selling it"

"No, by knocking off a wing."

"What?"

"Knocked down half the house. Ruined the symmetry."

"Why?"

"Grandfather was in the hospital, and she wanted to make it *cozier* for his return."

"You're kidding."

"No. I've seen it. Half a fine John Russell Pope Georgian, neatly and obscenely amputated. Gran said she didn't see the need for a ballroom anymore."

"God, I wouldn't mind a ballroom."

"They're crazy, aren't they?" Pearce says.

"And I thought it was just my mother."

"Nope. All crazy. The whole damn lot."

It's getting dark now; the lights from Beaufort are brighter as we walk back along the waterline.

"We're the same people, you know," says Pearce.

I turn, look at his face, try to read it. I ask, very simply: "How?"

"We've lost the same things."

It is not the answer I expect, but it pleases me. I do not think his words true; they are not. But I don't mind how he means them, not here in the dark.

The waves lap lightly at our feet. Looking down, I see the froth's strange green light.

"Look at the water," I say to Pearce.

"Phosphorus," he says.

"What's that?"

Pearce reaches down into the cold wet sand as the tide pulls away; he digs up a scoop with one finger.

"Here." He motions for me to hold out my hand, smooths the wet sand onto my palm.

I'm entranced by the green light. "It glows."

Pearce nods. I look down at the cold glowing sand, wanting to be fully appreciative of what is rare, what is in my hand.

We walk again, not talking. Eventually we find our shoes, the path we came on.

After dinner that night we take coffee. A civilized fire burns, and the living room smells of warm logs and furniture polish. Gilbert passes the tray of demitasse, which he leaves on the low table by the fire.

Pearce, Uncle Linc, and I rise quickly as Gran says good night, sparing us canasta. We resume our seats once she's disappeared down the hall.

Linc arrived just this morning. He's brought his springer spaniel, Bonnie, who waits by his feet as he takes sugar cubes from the coffee tray to dip into his Scotch. The fire crackles as Linc hand-feeds Bonnie the soaked cubes.

93

He turns his attention to us.

"You young people ever consider coming down by *train?*"

"You had a good trip?" says Pearce.

"Yes indeed. Hadn't been on a sleeper for a while. That's the way we used to come down. Yup, we had a good old time on that train. Especially when we got too old for Mrs. MacAully."

"Must have been fun," I say.

"Oh, *was*. We came down once without telling anybody, just us kids. It had been a while since Harry was home. I remember we sort of kidnapped the girls."

"So you four rode down together?" I ask.

"Five, actually," says Linc. "Colin Bennett was traveling with Harry. Good group of us. I was maybe twenty-one, your mother seventeen. We rode in adjoining compartments, stayed up most the night. I think that's the first time we ever got Sarah to take a drink."

"Really?"

"Oh, and that's when Colin really *noticed* Helen. Made perfect sense that she married him. He was the closest thing she could find to family. . . ." Linc pauses.

"Did you ever think about getting married?" I ask.

Linc laughs. "From my misspent years at the track, I know the odds."

"Of people divorcing?"

"No, of people *spawning!*" cries Linc. "I'd have to find a woman with an *incredibly* stable gene pool before I'd endanger society!"

Pearce explains. "You see, Linc thinks it's really quite chivalrous of him *not* to marry." He offers his uncle a conciliatory smile. "But his girlfriends never *quite* comprehend the nobility of his decision."

Linc laughs loudly at this. "I tell them I got bad blood," he says, crossing his arms. "And that they'd be crazy to want me. And although crazy women can be *mighty* attractive, I don't think I better have one any crazier than me."

Hours later I close my eyes and try to imagine the *clack-clack* of the rails, the chrome siding, and the small, close fixtures of the sleeping compartment. Helen and Mama would be sitting in matching robes on folded-down beds, Linc and Harry on the floor, pouring bourbon from silver flasks into small bathroom glasses. Young Helen drinking, that's easy to picture—cheeks flushed, laughing rosily. Mama is another matter. She'd be reticent, looking down in the semidark, contemplating the glass handed her, so full.

The next day Pearce and I drive into Beaufort for a matinee, James Bond.

At five we're heading back on Route 170. "Stagger Lee" is playing on the radio, and Pearce is singing along at a falsetto. "Stagger Lee, he shot Billy, shot him— Wait!" Pearce cries, interrupting himself.

He pulls the Morgan to the side of the road, then turns to look over his shoulder, back to the fireworks store. Near the border, there are a lot of these stores—small armories, really, South Carolina being one of the only states allowing the sale of serious fireworks.

"Let's get some," Pearce says.

"Why?" I ask.

"It's New Year's Eve."

The surprisingly large box of a building is constructed of white plastic siding. Inside, it's very bright—daylight shines through translucent walls, fluorescent tubes blaze from metal beams overhead. Pearce, in khakis and a riding jacket, stalks the aisles like a hunter, filling the red plastic basket with something from each shelf. He pulls down anything that catches his eye, looking for the biggest rockets but also choosing the things that delight me—gunpowder toys with names like Hen-Laying Egg, Pharaoh's Fountain, Magic Snakes.

"I think we have enough," I say.

"Grab me that blue . . ."

Finally, we work our way to the register. A man in a green Skoal cap and a chamois-cloth shirt slowly lifts each item as he punches in the price.

"You see, we're having a little trouble with the neighbors," Pearce jokes.

The man in the hat doesn't say anything, just looks at the labels, punches the keys.

"Two hundred and sixteen dollar, fifty-eight cent," he says, finally.

Pearce pays in cash.

"Good God, what trouble did you get into?" says Linc, who meets us in the mud room where we're sneaking in so that Gilbert won't see. Pearce holds out one of the shopping bags, and Linc pokes his nose down into it and then brings his head up slowly, returning a demonic smile.

"Your Gran's going to kill us."

"Gran's not going to know," Pearce says blithely.

"She always knows."

Pearce shrugs.

"You didn't get Snakes, did you?" asks Linc.

Pearce nods.

"They're hell to scrape off the flagstone." A small frown, Linc's banker face. "M-80s?"

Pearce nods quickly, his brows arched high, still grinning.

Linc says, "Remember, I had *nothing* to do with this."

For dinner it's Gran, Linc, Pearce, and myself. We have local oysters to start—platters and platters. The men have a contest to see who can eat the most. It's a draw, because Gran rings the secret buzzer under the rug near her foot, summoning Gilbert to clear.

A huge platter of venison follows. Gilbert holds steady as we take our fill. The girl follows him with silver dishes of brussels sprouts, mashed sweet potatoes, then black-eyed peas for New Year's, for luck.

Dessert is orange ambrosia, served with thick slices of pound cake. Gran can call up any number of things each morning at nine, propped in bed with a little porcelain menu card and a black wax pencil which she sends back to the kitchen with her tray. When grandchildren visit her room after breakfast, Gran says, "And what would *you* like for dessert?" You can order up pecan pie, lemon chess, peach cobbler, what-have-you.

Glass caddies at each end of the table hold chocolate-covered mint patties. Gran reaches for one, drops it in her water glass to chill. The rest of us follow.

At cards, the boys fidget. At ten-thirty Gran takes her leave.

Pearce and Linc plant the bottle launchers on the edge of the lawn, pointing over the marsh. Pearce is still in his dinner jacket, Linc's in shirtsleeves, as the two run up and down the edge of the drop, lighting fuses, then turning to watch the fiery showers arch over the water.

After half an hour Linc says he's tired and it's time for bed—he and Pearce are going out for duck at five-thirty the next morning. Pearce puts the leftover rockets in a paper bag and sets it on fire. We walk backward, shielding our eyes, as the bag begins to flame orange and blue. There are a few sputters and then loud cracks as the first of the larger rockets hiss skyward. We keep walking backward as the flame grows, turning green, then starting explosions rat-a-tat-tat like machine gun fire. The noise is terrific. God help the lawn.

Pearce tells me I've turned out remarkably well, considering.

It's after midnight of the new year; he and I sit deep in the sofa by the fire. He gets up occasionally to stoke the logs or fix a drink. He smells of smoke.

"No, I mean really," he says, when I laugh and try to look offended. "You could have turned out very strangely, being kept on that place all those years."

By "that place," Pearce means my mother's farm in Oregon, the socialist concept. Pearce chooses to be a staunch conservative in a family of Democrats—makes dinner conversation livelier. Not that Gran or Linc or Helen were hot on the commune idea. Noblesse oblige stopped long before that.

"But now you're really civilized," he adds.

"Thank you," I say, curt but not cold.

Pearce pours me a small glass of Chinese liqueur he brought down from New York. The first sip burns my throat, but the rest follows easily. I tilt my head back, arching my neck as I swallow, making the burn last longer.

We speak of many things. Pearce tells me about quality, about how he used to want to open a store that sold only the best of everything—the best jam, the best horse blankets, the best evening slippers. Damn it, he says, people have been bothersome, asking him what he planned to do. He shakes his head and says:

"It's a pity that retail's so tacky."

"Retail's tacky?" I ask. "What about Great-Great-Grandfather?"

Pearce scrunches up his face. "Well, he *was* tacky, but he was so good at it the rest of us don't have to be."

"Don't have to be what?" I ask. "Tacky or good at something?"

For an instant Pearce considers. Then says:

"Both."

"Maybe real estate," Pearce says. "I could live six months of the year in Palm Beach, sell one great big tacky house a year and call it a business. I'd get a really great office."

"What about a real job?" I ask. "Or graduate school?"

"I expect I'll be too busy."

"No, seriously . . ."

"Hah! You just wait till *you're* twenty-one and have to manage your own money."

Pearce tells me to come to New York after graduation, that he'll make me a present of the best weekend ever. "But you must come in May. All the good parties are over by June."

"But I have exams then. . . ."

"Or Bastille Day! Bastille Day will be wonderful! You must come up for Bastille Day. . . ."

I agree.

Pearce looks down at my hand. "You bite your nails, don't you?"

"Yes." I pull my hand back.

"You should stop."

"I'm trying. . . ."

"Not hard enough." He keeps my hand.

He does not say, "Look at me," but we are both staring, which is not like us, not like us separately. I am staring at him as directly as if he were a mirror; our gaze is level, our expressions match. Neither one of us moves.

Slowly, eyes not shifting, he lifts his free hand to my face. Lightly, he touches my cheek. I arch my neck so that my face caresses his hand, my eyes avert his.

Neither of us acknowledges the small movements.

His hand glazes my neck, my shoulder, my collarbone. Our eyes meet again.

We study each other in detail. His eyes are the palest, clearest green, with dark, dark lashes. The fire bakes his tan skin rosy. It is hot where we are sitting. He smells of wood smoke and liqueur, gunpowder from the rockets. It is so quiet that our breath seems very loud, as does the ticking of the clock, the hiss and fizzle of the fire.

I know the fascination behind this. His skin feels like mine. But it's going too far.

His hand is again against my cheek. I smell the crisp starch of his shirt.

He passes one finger over my lips, half open. I try to draw in a breath, but there is no air—what's there seems thin, warm, used up.

I shiver and break.

But he is still staring steady.

"What?" he says.

"Nothing," I say, still not looking.

"It's like looking in a mirror, isn't it?"

His hand is still at my cheek. The heat is too much. I feel my stomach turn.

"No," I say.

"Then what is it like?"

I draw in a clear breath, wait, then say:

"I think I should say good night."

To my surprise, his hand drops. "Good night, then." With that he rises and, with a formal nod, waits for me. I rise hurriedly. He waits for me to walk out, then follows. At the base of the stairs he stops and says, again:

"Good night."

I climb the stairs and look down to where he's standing, formally, impossible to read.

That night, in my bed, I press my cheek against the smooth cool laundered pillowcase and again catch the smell of starch. My stomach tightens, uneasy. I turn over to face the ceiling, draw the comforter up, but it doesn't help. I still smell the starch and wonder how I'll ever get to sleep.

VISITS

Connecticut, April 1, 1986

Supposedly, my mother's worst memories involved standing in the doorway at Chapin, waiting for the other girls to leave before she'd run out to the waiting limousine.

I did not expect to have such compunctions.

At eleven, a discreet navy-blue sedan pulls in front of the dining hall. I'm waiting out on the steps, dressed in a black-watch-plaid jumper with a white portrait-collar blouse underneath. I'm wearing new black pumps with a one-inch heel, my hair is smoothed back beneath a velvet band.

I rise as George gets out. "Miss Meredith?" I nod and pick up my bag, which he hurries to take from me.

"Very swish," I hear from behind. Mr. Day, college adviser, looking amused.

From the car, pulling out of the circle onto the main drive, I see Dean Harvey's work squad. Two boys in jeans, two still in coat and tie, all with rakes and black plastic garbage bags. Mr. Harvey's standing in front of them, holding a stack of folders and a clipboard, his stomach poking beyond his madras blazer.

I lean back in the seat and slouch low, hidden by the doorjamb.

Westport's not the same, because it was never Grandfather's. The house is a fair size, four bedrooms, usually empty since Helen's bought a house five minutes away. The grounds seem small only when compared to Broadhurst.

We sit in the living room before lunch. Gran reads her book. Helen offers a drink, and I say no.

White-haired Sylvie comes in with a plate of broiled Wheat Thins wrapped in bacon. We're waiting for Pearce to arrive before we eat.

This room is painted the same butter yellow as Gran's New York apartment. There are several sofas banked with pillows and many small scattered tables to hold drinks and ashtrays. On the mantel stands a strangely modern bronze of a horse, flanked by blue Chinese vases.

The bay window provides a wide view to the formal gardens, the duck pond, the neglected tennis court. The tree at the window has just started to bud. One dry limb scratches against the glass as a bird lights. Warm, still sunshine pours across Guinness, who lies at Helen's feet. She bends down every few minutes to stroke him behind the ears. A modish pendant on a silk rope swings from her neck as she does this. On the stroking hand Helen wears a stack of Barry Kieselstein-Cord rings. Otherwise she's in a navy-blue cashmere turtleneck and matching trousers, navy snaffle-bit Guccis on her feet.

She and Gran are drinking these terrible drinks made with bouillon and vodka. Bullshots, they're called.

Helen reaches down beside her chair and lifts a book, a current biography. She opens it and removes a clipping from behind the cover.

"Did you see this, Meredith?"

I nod yes. It ran in a Manhattan real estate magazine.

"When she wears her hair like that, I could swear it was me before I married—what do you think, Mum?" Helen passes the clipping to Gran.

"And who is this, dear?" Gran asks.

Helen leans in and speaks to Gran's better ear.

"It's Meredith, Mum. With Pearce."

The photo was taken at a museum party in New York. I was ostensibly on a college visit. I'm in a borrowed black dress, Pearce to my left.

Helen says, "Doesn't she look like me at her age, all done up like that?"

Gran turns the clipping over, feeling the paper between her fingers. She looks up at me and then down at the picture, a slight disapproving look.

I hold my breath.

"Meredith and Pearce," says Gran. "Yes, I see it printed." She looks at me again, enjoying her pause, then says with finality, "Sometimes good to be in print, sometimes not."

———

I don't know what they know, how much they know. The last time I saw Pearce was in Florida, in March.

I'd been at Helen's for a week. Her club was separated

from the mainland by two narrow bridges; trunks of cypress twisting over the road, white petrified timber strangled by vines.

The first six days I took tennis lessons and each night ate at the club with Helen and her friends.

Pearce arrived Saturday for the spring dance. I had another dress from Helen's Philippe—blush-colored satin with a crinoline underskirt that swayed like a bell when I walked.

Light rain sounded on the tent roof, letting up. The night air was humid, causing my hair to curl at the temples. I patted it down as I moved back from Freddy.

The band paused to light clapping.

"Thank you," Freddy said, nodding politely.

Mike Carney played "Luck Be a Lady Tonight," as Helen sat smoking Camels with an aging German writer whom Pearce referred to as old Sour Kraut.

It had started off nicely. Pearce and I sat at a table near Helen's. My cousin hadn't asked me to dance—he rarely danced—but he'd seemed proud of me, making jokes, everything seeming fine.

An hour later Pearce's cream linen jacket was off and he reclined lazily on a deck chair down by the pool. He had one leg on and one leg off the chaise, his arms crossed behind his head. This pose accommodated a girl who sat perched upright, turning her head in conversation with him. The girl wore a long dress in an old blue and green Pucci print, which bared her shoulders and back. Pale hair ran thin and straight down the exposed skin.

"Let's dance," I'd said to Freddy Johnson, sitting to my left.

Across the dance floor I'd watched the row of deck chairs.

The band launched into a faster set of songs, forcing

gaiety on the evening. Couples in their middle years filled the floor, and my view of Pearce was blocked.

When Freddy had danced me to a position from which I could see, Pearce and the Pucci girl were walking down the wooden plankway to the beach. The girl's long blue and green swirled skirt rippled and flapped above the grey planks that led to the sand. From up above I'd watched as she bent down to unstrap her high silver sandals. She stood on one foot, her hand on Pearce's arm for balance.

I was still dancing with Freddy when Pearce reappeared.

He nodded to the guests at Helen's table, leaned and gave his mother a quick kiss on the cheek before walking, hands in pockets, toward the door.

"Excuse me," I said to Freddy. "I've got to see about my ride home."

"Well, I can—"

But I was gone, pretending not to hear.

It was like watching myself from a distance as I did this.

Quick steps—around the tent stake, the sodden rope, the edge of tautly drawn canvas. The grass was wet but the rain had stopped as I cut across the lawn, catching up.

Almost running, I reached him under the arch by the glass cabinets—photos from the fifties, golf winners with trophies. I tapped his arm. "Pearce?"

Pearce turned and looked straight at me—it was as if he didn't know me. He kept walking.

It occurred to me that I had no idea what to say, very little idea of what I'd done wrong.

I moved behind him on the balls of my feet, so my heels didn't clack on the parquet as I followed him through the club, under the long awning to the drive. He nodded

*to a green-coated valet and stood stock-still with his hands
in his pockets, face lit in profile by the low lampposts. He
knew I was back there.*

"Pearce!" I called.

Nothing.

"Pearce!"

He turned around.

Bright morning sun glared off the ocean and poured
under the half-closed blind. I remember these in my line
of vision: pink scalloped-edged guest towels, marble soap-
dish holding pink Floris soap, and, above the sink, a large
white mirror paved with seashells. I studied my reflection.

Small marks lay scattered on my neck and shoulders.
Odd blue bruises from the point of a tooth.

"Don't you see it's the only way?" he'd said, windows
fogged with breath. "Don't you see we're all there is?"

I studied my neck. Blanket-white skin, with a blue
cast to the two faintly raised arteries. I tilted my head to
the mirror and examined the pea-sized bruises. Then,
pushing my shoulders back, I noticed how high my collarbone appeared, noticed the full length of my neck—
high and straight. Something cold and proud rose, something I didn't immediately recognize.

I stood there on the white bath mat and just looked.

———

It's one-thirty when Sylvie comes into the living room
and says that Pearce has called to cancel, that he's had car
trouble outside Trenton. We finally sit down to lunch.

"That's been happening a lot," says Helen. "I'm thinking perhaps he needs a new car."

"Thought that was a new car," says Gran.

• • •

George drives me back to school. In the evening it starts to snow.

I study with the clock radio on low.

"Freaky April," says the WHCN deejay, "but if you don't like the weather, just wait ten minutes."

At eleven I turn off the light and go to bed.

I wake to a gentle rap on the door. "Yes?" I sit up.

Lydia pokes her head around the door, blond bangs and the white eyelet ruffle of her Lanz nightgown lit from the hallway behind her.

"It's him again." Lydia's the other corridor prefect and has the room across from the phone.

I look at the clock. Two in the morning. "God, Lydia, I'm sorry."

The first time Pearce phoned after lights-out, Lydia said, "Oh, please, no problem. We had fun talking. He knows this guy my sister dated."

And I said something like: "Still, I'm sorry it's so late."

And she said, "Tell him to come visit. Tell him we all saw his picture and we think he's hot."

But tonight she says, "He wants to talk to you. He's in a stairwell. In what sounds from his description to be Cushing Hall."

"*Our* Cushing Hall?"

"Yes."

"Oh, no."

"You want to talk to him?"

"God, no."

"Well then, what should I say?"

"Tell him to go away. Tell him I'd like to graduate."

"O.K."

Lydia disappears down the corridor, returns thirty seconds later.

"He wants to see you. I told him that was impossible."

"Certainly is."

"He wanted to know which dorm we were in," Lydia says.

"You didn't tell him, I hope."

"Shouldn't you talk to him?"

"No. Leave the phone off the hook."

We shut the door to the corridor so that no light comes in, and we peer out onto the quad. A set of headlights beam through the softly falling flakes (a thick, wet snow).

There's engine noise and a soft crunching as the car moves slowly around the circle, leaving dark tire tracks.

"He should cut his lights," says Lydia as we watch.

A light goes on across the quad in Memorial House.

"That's the McNeils' apartment," whispers Lydia. Then a hush. Mr. McNeil stands at his window, silhouetted black as he watches the car.

We crouch down at the windowsill, though we can't be seen through the dark. The radiator blows hot at our necks and hands, where nightgowns don't cover. The window's fogged, slightly wet from our breathing.

The car stops on the drive in front of the dorm. One flight down and to the right of my window, the front doorway is lit. Lydia and I can see Pearce clearly as he walks the length of the building. He's wearing a blazer with jeans but no topcoat, his pink oxford is unbuttoned at the neck. He has his hands in his pockets and moves hurriedly in the snow, in short, little hops—his shoes must be wet.

We duck down. When we look up he's stopped about thirty feet left of my window and is looking straight up in front of him.

"What's he doing?" Lydia whispers.

His hands are bare, no gloves. He digs into his pocket, throws something up against a window.

"*Damn*, that's *my* room," says Lydia. "I left my light on."

"He must think it's mine."

Faintly, we hear the gentle pings against glass. He throws coins until he runs out.

"Maybe you should talk to him," says Lydia.

"No."

"You are such a *bitch*."

After a minute Pearce steps back, still watching the window. A dark patch of muddy ground remains where he stood—the snow trampled, melted.

But he doesn't turn back toward his car. Instead, he turns left, disappearing around the corner.

"Oh, God."

We hear clanging as he tries the side door. But it's locked, as it should be.

Pearce walks back into view, surveying the dorm.

A door bangs shut across the quad. Mr. McNeil stands in the lighted doorway of Memorial House, his arms crossed.

Pearce glances over at him, ambles back to his car. As he gets in, he gives Mr. McNeil a little wave of acknowledgment.

"Did he just *wave?*" says Lydia.

"You'd better get back to your room. McNeil will check up," I say.

But Mr. McNeil just stands and watches the car lights

fade. After a minute he walks back into Memorial House. His apartment goes dark.

"Why'd he do that?" Lydia asks.

"Probably figures he's scared him away."

"No, not McNeil . . . your *cousin*. What's with him?"

"Hard to say." And so I tell her the story, edited. We sit whispering in the dark, a roll of slice-and-bake cookie dough from Lydia's contraband fridge disappearing in small chunks between us.

I thought Pearce would call the next day, call and say, "God, I was on a tear the other night." But he doesn't. He doesn't call again that spring.

Felicity calls at the end of May to ask how my exams are going, mentions that Pearce and Princeton have seen fit to part ways. "Quite mutual, I believe," is what she says.

Felicity says that she would love to come for my graduation but that she's leaving June 1 with some horses for Europe.

"My recent professional status has my mother more riled than Pearce's dropout. Funny, that."

—

The first William P. Fraser never went to college. At fourteen, he went to Chicago. This was just before the Civil War.

Great-Great-Grandfather swept floors at Pearson's Dry Goods for a dollar a week. When the older boys went to war, he was promoted to manager. By night he read borrowed books by the light of an oil lamp.

He put his name on his own store in 1870. By 1890 his name was synonymous with the city's.

The most famous family story is from Chicago, circa 1905. It seems that there was a salon that catered only to the best women. Mrs. William Pearce Fraser, Grandfather's grandmother, had a standing appointment. When she arrived, she saw that her usual seat was occupied by Mrs. Armour. So Great-Great-Grandmother nodded to the attendant and very sweetly said:

"Get the butcher's wife out of my chair."

The first William P. Fraser died in 1910. The afternoon of his funeral, they shut down the Chicago Stock Exchange. His State Street competitors closed their doors as shoppers and employees spilled out onto the sidewalks to watch the slow procession of black-draped carriages that traveled from the mansion on Prairie Avenue to pass the storefront.

A nephew took over the business, as the first William Fraser no longer had a son and his grandson was but a boy.

Chicago was a good town, but too small for the third William Fraser. After Eton and Oxford, Grandfather thought it time for New York.

PART II

AT GRAN'S

I walk past the Carlyle on my way home to Gran's. The day is windy and cold. For the first time, I notice heating coils underneath the hotel's awning. They glow orange red, warming guests as they walk to waiting cars, but warming passersby as well.

When I enrolled at Columbia I considered the dorms, but they're on 116th Street, and it's not as if they don't charge you. My father would worry if I lived in Harlem, so to spare him that and the expense I stay at Gran's on Seventy-sixth. ("I'll be four blocks from the Met," I'd told my father. "More like four from Ralph Lauren," he replied.)

So my New York is different from that of my classmates. I ride the bus home amid the schoolgirls who live on Park; they wear sloppy sweaters with uniform skirts and blucher moccasins, carry French book bags with the flap open. I have a charge at Zitomer Pharmacy, where the window display holds boar-bristle brushes, satin hair ornaments, Chanel powders. Sylvie comes in twice a week to clean, brings me covered dishes with warming instructions. For me, living in the city is like standing underneath the awning at the Carlyle—warm and sheltered.

Gran hasn't been in the apartment for over a year. In the warm months she stays in Connecticut, but with the cold goes down to Heyton Hall, leaving me Sylvie. I do try to keep the place neat. It's actually more of a strain than if there were no one, cleaning the place before Sylvie arrives.

The apartment's in pales—mostly creams and yellows, the furnishings lighter and more feminine than those in the Connecticut house. There are Staffordshire dogs on the mantel, porcelain birds on small scattered tables. In the corner there's a round bridge table covered by a cream cloth with the bottom edge fringed and tasseled. It seems strange to me that the cards and tally sheets are out, in the center, as if Gran's home and expecting friends. ("Dead. I no longer play bridge because my bridge friends are dead," she said from her chair in Connecticut.)

My room has wallpaper with a pattern of white lilacs; on the bed is an old-fashioned silk and lace cover. Between the curtained windows is a skirted vanity table, in the back of the closet, on padded hangers, hang Gran's extra evening things—foreign caftans in jewel tones, all gifts from Helen. Below the far window, a painted grille hides an old-fashioned radiator. It hisses at night, which sometimes wakes me, but I hear the heat is broken in the dorms, so I can't complain.

• • •

Gran had a rule about the apartment: no grandchildren. But that had been aimed at Pearce, who'd given a party there when he was seventeen.

Pearce called me in September. He was passing through.

"I heard about your coup," he said.

"How do you mean?"

"You're staying at Seventy-sixth Street. You know *I'm* not allowed to stay at Seventy-sixth Street."

"Maybe there's a reason for that."

Cooing: "Euuuh, isn't our little Meredith well behaved?"

He was getting a group together for lunch that day. Since finishing with Princeton—or Princeton with him—Pearce had been traveling.

I couldn't have lunch, I told him. I had a class.

"What a good girl," he said.

"How long are you in town?" I asked.

"Till this evening probably. Look, I've gotta run."

A few days later I saw him from across Madison. He was sitting at an outside table at Le Relais with a red-haired girl I knew from the papers as Lulu. The wind came up and rustled her hair as she pulled it back over one shoulder, raking at the roots with her fingers. Pearce wore charcoal pinstripes and rested his elbows on the tablecloth in just the right way. I didn't feel up to saying hello.

Saturday. Helen's in from the country to see a show at the Met. She brings by the exhibition catalog. The cover photo is of a carriage from the Prince of Liechtenstein's collection: gilded, with painted panels by Boucher.

Sylvie makes us lunch at the apartment, setting the card table formally: Baccarat, salt dishes, fish forks.

117

"I like eating here at the card table," says Helen. "It was your mother's idea to set lunch here; she felt the dining room too *formal.*"

"I thought Gran got this place in the early seventies."

"She did. Nineteen seventy-three? Moved up from Seventy-second Street, Lord knows why. The duplex was ever so much nicer."

"But you said my mother was here?"

"Yes. For at least a week, as I remember." Sylvie brings in a tray of crab salad, Helen serves herself without looking up. "Sylvie, do you remember Sarah's visit?"

"Ah, yes. Mrs. Scott, she was here just after the work on the kitchen finished."

"She'd just been at some yoga center," says Helen. "Wait, no, I think it was an island. Yes, in Micronesia, that was it."

"She was so tired," says Sylvie. "She sleep long time, keep shades down even when she awake."

Helen nods. "I came in from Paris to see her, and we couldn't go out. She'd only brought sandals and batik islandwear—can you imagine landing at Kennedy like that in the dead of winter? Anyway, we ate here."

"I thought Mama hadn't seen Gran," I say.

"Winter, dear. Where do you think your Gran would be?"

"Oh. That's right."

Sylvie finishes serving and disappears. Aunt Helen continues:

"But we had such a nice visit. Your mother was trying to decide where to go next. I dropped off some sweaters and a pair of warm boots for her, hoping that maybe this time she wouldn't go quite so far."

"I never knew about this."

"Well, she didn't want your father to find her, or you to worry."

"She didn't want us to *worry?*"

"You didn't, did you?"

"I suppose not." I really couldn't remember.

"You got used to her being gone."

"No. On the farm, when she was there . . ." There were some good times on the farm, when she wasn't sick. I think, then say: "It was more like I thought nothing bad could happen to her, really."

"Nine lives," says Helen. She pauses, looking behind me. "I think those curtains have seen better days, don't you?"

"They seem fine."

"I haven't liked them from the start. Maybe it's time to start fresh." Helen takes a small bite from her fork. "Sylvie's peas are good, aren't they? I usually hate peas, but she uses masses of butter. Lord help me if there's dessert."

There is, of course.

We don't talk anymore about my mother.

———

Barbara doesn't talk about her unless I ask. When I do, it goes something like this:

"I think it was Nancy Phillips who called her 'the most beautiful mouse in the world.' Your mother was completely oblivious to her looks. At Radcliffe she wore the simplest cotton dresses, no jewelry, and her hair always looked just combed, though you'd never see her touch it. Now and then she'd put on some lipstick that Helen had given her, and that would be it. But you have to remember we didn't get out of the library much."

                                    •   •   •

All Papa will say:

"She was perfection."

When I repeat this to Barbara, she raises her brow:

*"She had sweet features, so acquaintances would
credit her with a sweet disposition, to which I'd say 'Hah!'
and leave it at that. Your father remained fooled, and I
mean that in the nicest way. The first time they met was
at Nancy Phillips'. Sarah was sitting cross-legged in tennis
shorts on a grand Persian rug. That would have been 1962.
We were all in Cambridge for summer session, would go
over to Nancy's because it was so hot in our little flat. We
kept the window open all the time, but the gauze curtains
wouldn't move—no breeze. That summer we lived on
tuna fish and Russian novels.*

*"Mornings, your mother would go to the Radcliffe
courts to play tennis with your father. They played
early, to beat the heat. But tennis was all it was for
a while. At least for her. Until that spring when Harry
died."*

There is a photo my father took when he came to Mississippi to visit my mother and me:

*. . . Outside the dirty trailer, sitting on cement blocks,
a red gasoline can beside us. Mama's smiling, her hair flat
to her head and the center part uneven. I'm in Oshkosh
overalls, she's in filthy corduroy pants. You can actually
see dirt on my mother's nose, a big smudge. She's got a
Band-Aid on one finger, her wedding ring still on the
other. Besides the ring, one thing makes it clear she's the
same woman—sheer pink frosted lipstick she'd put on for
my father. But I don't know that for sure. Maybe the ring*

                                    120

and the lipstick were what a white woman needed in rural Mississippi, in the midst of tension, to draw attention to distinctions she'd meant to break down.

Anyway, my father used the photo as evidence. A court order had us back in California the following week. It was the dirt that did it.

GRAVEL DRIVES

New York, February 1988

It rains Sunday afternoon, grey rivers down Gran's windows. I huddle under a blanket, watching *The Razor's Edge* on the old black-and-white Zenith.

The story opens shortly after the First World War.

Gene Tierney perches on the low stone wall of the country club, away from the music. She has an orchid pinned at her waist.

Tyrone Power is back from the war. Tierney pleads with him to remain in Chicago. "There are many opportunities for a young man. The Armours and the Swifts will pack more and better meat, the McCormicks will produce more and better harvesters."

Tyrone Power looks past her, over the low wall to where the lake glistens in the dark.

The girl continues, with conviction: "This is a young country, and it is a young man's responsibility to take part in its progress."

He continues to gaze into the distance.

This was Grandfather's era—he fought in that war, an officer with the First Illinois Cavalry. But when he returned he had no call for Chicago or for country clubs.

That evening I receive a call from Gordon Emerson.

"Hey—I'm in New York!" he says. "Just drove in!"

"Great!"

We talk a bit.

"So what brings you to town?" I ask.

"A paper. 'Gold Coast Gothic.' I'm here to look at Court Hill."

"Where's that?"

"Near Huntington."

"Oh. When are you doing that?"

"Tomorrow. But I thought I'd come back to the city tomorrow night."

"So you're driving out to Long Island tomorrow?"

"Yeah. Why? Want to go?"

"Not if I'd get in the way of your work . . ."

"No, I've just got to take a few pictures and . . . Wait. Broadhurst is yours, right?"

"I wouldn't say mine."

"I know, I know. But it's a John Russell Pope, correct?"

"You've seen it?"

"In photos, not in life."

"Neither have I."

"Well . . . Want to?"

———

Most of the pictures I've seen were in a magazine article. Several years ago, Pearce brought a volume of 1934 Country Life *to Maine (twelve issues bound in black leather, "P.U. Library" stamped as warning throughout). Amid articles on children's ponies, rose hybrids, and house presents (Saks offered a chromium-plated cocktail set during Prohibition) ran a six-page piece punned "William Fraser's English Manor."*

The black-and-white photos were shot to show maximum breadth and width. The first was of the main house, enormous and Georgian, with vast rolled lawns stretching grandly in either direction. Beyond this lay Long Island Sound—great cliffs dropping off to the beach, the perfect vista.

The text lauded the woods stocked with pheasants, the tennis pavilion, the docked yacht and speedboats, the guest cottages, the guests. There was a photo of the oval swimming pool, captioned as "emerald green." It had a graceful marble curve, shallow shaded steps and a Palladian bathhouse.

There were photos of the famous racing stables— Georgian brick built around a central court with a clock tower, round Adam windows, all the fixtures in solid brass. The dairy barn was also pictured—a pretty Cotswold design holding eighty prize guernseys. The watchmen's cottages had leaded casements borrowed from Grandfather's memories of Oxford. The other outbuildings included a dairy plant to process milk, cream, and butter not just for the main house but for the house and grounds staff. Also mentioned were vast greenhouses, goose, pig, and hen houses, a hospital barn for sick cattle, an electrical plant. The point of all this being that Grandfather's Broadhurst could function independently, answering to no one.

—

Gordon exits at Oyster Bay and takes 25A through Lloyd Harbor. A white sign points to Broadhurst State Park.

Within minutes we reach a wooden tollbooth. A small grey man in a flannel shirt nods. "Parking's to the left."

"We'd like to see the main house, please," I say. "I believe it's still quite a drive from here."

"Can't let you drive there. Roads are for walking. Ain't but one and three-quarter mile."

The road is paved in black asphalt. Gordon and I walk, bundled up, the cold mild for February.

We pass through fawn-colored fields, bare witchy trees. We pass two older men walking in nylon sweatsuits and Reeboks. One smokes a cigar and wears his hair greased.

We stop to look at the Cotswold dairy barns, but they are padlocked, the windows boarded, light graffiti on one door.

The black asphalt takes us through pine forest.

"I'd heard these roads were gravel," I say.

Gordon nods. "Probably were. You won't see gravel used that way anymore. An extraordinary amount of labor went into raking them, maintaining them. At my great-grandfather's place they had a crew out every morning at dawn."

Coming over the hill, we see the main house in the distance. We stop.

"What do you think?" says Gordon.

Keeping in mind that this is winter, I am still struck by the bleakness. Most of the windows are bare, while a few frame the awkward outlines of makeshift curtains, a pull blind at half mast.

"It looks different from photographs," I murmur.

"Well, the left half of it *is* missing."

"Gran thought that would make it cozier. . . ." I stand, staring.

Gordon snorts and shakes his head. "Hah."

"What do you mean?" I ask.

"Death and taxes, Meredith, death and taxes." He clucks his tongue and walks purposefully ahead.

There are two vans parked in front. A young bearded man sits on the stone steps, making notes on a clipboard.

"Hello," says Gordon, friendly.

"Hi there."

"I'm Gordon Emerson, and this is Meredith Scott."

"And I'm Jeff. . . . May I help you?"

"We were wondering if we could possibly please see the house," I say.

"Her mother grew up here," adds Gordon.

The man brightens.

"Here? Cool."

I smile and shrug meekly.

"I've been living here two years now," says Jeff. "Guess it looks pretty different. Must have been neat, though, for her."

I nod with a tight smile.

"Well," says Jeff, "we're between sessions now. But by all means look around."

Jeff follows us as we do.

The great hall is painted white.

"In photos this was a darker color," I say.

"It was white when I got here," says Jeff. "Needs another coat, I'd say."

All of the large rooms on the first floor are painted white. It is hard to tell their original purpose. Scattered folding chairs and a classroom table are dwarfed by these high open spaces, these wide pageant rooms.

Jeff clears his throat. "Our next session will be a fifth-grade group from Queens. They're studying ecosystems. I organize meals and whatnot."

"I'd heard that this was a school for the blind," I say.

"Briefly. They do what they can with the place."

Gordon examines the molding, the arch of a doorway.

"May I see the bedrooms?" I ask.

Jeff takes us upstairs to a dormlike hallway painted hospital green. He opens a door to reveal metal bunk beds and institutional furniture. The floor is carpeted with brown shag fragments, poorly fitted, overlapping.

"Can I see more of the rooms?" I ask.

"All the bedrooms are alike," says Jeff.

"Do you know which was the children's wing?"

"No. I think these might have been guest rooms. Would you like to see the view from the roof?"

We follow Jeff up more stairs, down a low hallway, through a closet narrowing into a crawl space. A door opens at the end of the passage to reveal a high, light-filled room.

"The skylight oculus," says Jeff proudly, as Gordon examines the control wires leading to a glassed opening above.

We follow Jeff up more stairs, then out onto the roof. "Well. This is it," he says.

"Thank you," I say.

Jeff stands silent for a moment, then leaves us to our

bleak view of the cliffs, the grey winter sea. At this height the ocean wind is strong and bitter.

"I don't see the poolhouse."

"They probably tore it down," says Gordon. "They don't want the vandals hurting themselves and suing."

We're quiet for a bit. I turn and walk to the other side, the view of the fields and drive. I can see the stable steeple in the distance.

"My mother's friend Barbara," I say, "wanted to set a book here."

"What happened?"

"She got one chapter into it, then realized it wouldn't work. She said it sounded too much like a fairy tale, the brothers Grimm."

"Really."

"Funny. It doesn't strike me that way."

Gordon puts his hand against my back, against the cold.

Jeff reappears. "Enough?" he asks.

"Enough."

That evening Gordon delivers me back to Gran's, where I fix him a plate of pasta. Then he goes out to meet his friends—I'm too tired.

In bed, I imagine the halls before the sale, before the bunk beds and the paint. A wing would have been shut off from lack of use, white drop cloths hanging over armoires and bureaus, transforming chairs, now missing, into ghosts. I have a vivid vision of a carved mahogany foot emerging from beneath a drop cloth, a griffin's claw—clenched and gothic—curling round a scepter.

And out the window, half boarded, the rolled green lawns and open spaces.

FAIRY

DUST

Avon, Connecticut,
March 1988

"The boys' governess, Mrs. MacAully, and the girls' nanny, Margaret, were always feuding. That's one of the reasons we rarely saw the boys. Then Mrs. MacAully got sick, and I remember we were glad."

I'm at Barbara's for the weekend, two hours by train. It's dark and wet outside, a steady drum of rain. The kitchen's lit by candles, we're sitting at the pine table with a large bowl of popcorn tossed with chunks of butter and grated Parmesan. Barbara continues:

"One afternoon Margaret took the five of us to the movies to see *Peter Pan*. Later that night we snuck down to the boys' sitting room and talked about the movie,

129

played out parts. Harry was Peter, of course, and Helen was Wendy. Do you remember the story?"

I nod yes.

"There's that scene in the movie where they bounce on the bed—that's how they begin to fly. After we bounced higher and higher the boys gave Helen a dare; she jumped off and twisted her ankle. The nanny woke from the noise and was running in the door when it happened. Harry said, 'It's 'cause we forgot the fairy dust.' And Helen said, 'Send Margaret for some.'"

"Wasn't Helen in pain?" I ask.

"She didn't complain, though I'm sure it swelled up later. With all that comfort around them, that family went to the damnedest lengths to find ways to hurt themselves. Wore casts and splints like medals."

"So Helen thought she could fly?"

"Well, there was that sense at Broadhurst, that wishes were instantly granted."

I ask about the nannies, the distant children's wing— the reasons. Barbara thinks a minute before answering.

"It was part of the era," she says. "I'd say that the girls' mother was, considering the way things were, quite attentive. If we children felt uncomfortable around her, it wasn't out of anything she did—not consciously. I've told you about how your Gran would drive us herself to horse shows, haven't I? Your mother, Helen, and me. The horse trailer would've gone on ahead, sometimes with your mother, wanting to be with her babies. Late one afternoon after a show we stopped at a drugstore—the old-fashioned kind with the painted sign hanging out front and a freezer with a sliding glass top, ice cream bars. Well, your grandmother bought us push pops and sugar cones—the kind

130

that's chocolate and nuts on top, under a spiral peel wrapper? Your Gran was good that way, letting young girls have chocolate. My mother wouldn't let me eat it—bad for the skin. *Anyway,* we sat on the steps of this store, unwrapping our ice creams. There was Mrs. William Fraser III, sitting on the ground, neatly eating her push pop with a napkin. So it's not like she *wouldn't* sit down on the floor; it's just that her usual circumstances didn't allow for it."

"What about Grandfather?"

"Your grandfather? He was a wonderful man."

"But what do you remember the most?"

"Well, let's see. . . . There were some fall mornings, when he was still healthy, that he'd take Sarah out cubbing. I was staying out at Broadhurst once when they did this, sleeping in a room down the hall from Sarah's. Those halls were so long and dark, but maybe everything seemed bigger and scarier at that age. Sarah said the night before that she was going cubbing early and to go down for breakfast without her. There was no question of me going along—not because I was a bad rider, but because this was clearly her time alone with her father. . . ."

"Cubbing?"

"Riding around looking for batches of fox cubs—signs of a litter, whatever those were. Basically a nice morning ride, watching things grow. From my window I saw them returning—your grandfather silver and handsome, his riding clothes perfect; Sarah in full kit, perfectly straight on Hadrian. It was cold, and I could see fogs of breath rising, marking their gentle country talk. I felt very glad for her that she had that."

"Me too."

Barbara looks at me. "Parents in our day were different. There was less expected of them. But your mother's did better than their contemporaries. Better than mine." She pauses. "Or so it seemed to me, back then."

———

There's a photo of the living room at Broadhurst, taken, say, 1958.

It's evening—the men are in dinner jackets and the women in long skirts, with crisply waved hair. Grandfather's leaning back, comfortable, his arm looped over the backrest, Helen at his side. He's got this slick look, hair silver at the sides, Persian cat color, which it had been since his satiny-smooth playboy days. Heavy eyelids droop urbanely as he looks without expression to the center of the room, where a young male houseguest stands on one foot, acting out a charade. Only Linc and Barbara lean forward, gesticulating, trying to solve the puzzle.

———

The popcorn is down to burnt kernels. We sip chamomile tea from brown earthenware mugs. Little slicks of honeycomb wax float melted on top.

Barbara says, "*Yes*, I'd say the girls sought approval from Harry. Especially after their father died. But being grown-up young ladies, the stakes were different. Ball dresses, a quick line. Your mother never thought herself good at that, so she never tried to compete. She was too serious, such a grind at college, struggling miserably with premed, dying to be a vet. But then she decided she didn't have the grades and changed her major to English. At that point we were hearing even less of Harry. He was always traveling."

I ask how my mother reacted when Broadhurst was sold.

"I don't think she missed it one bit. She didn't talk about these things easily, but I do remember her saying when she was older, married: 'The thing I disliked most about that house was that whenever you'd get up from a chair, a footman would appear out of nowhere to plump the cushions.' It was as if she made no impression at all."

I ask about Helen. Barbara considers, then answers delicately.

"I'm not sure if Helen missed that house, although I know she was angry your Gran sold it for a song. There were things that had bothered Helen too."

"Like what?"

"Well, occasionally, until she was grown, Helen would sleepwalk. The powers that be put bars on her windows to protect her. But I know it made her feel queer—window bars were associated with crazy people."

I pause, finally ask, "When is it, do you think, that Helen went crazy?"

Barbara studies me carefully before asking, "Is Helen crazy?"

I nod, surprised with myself.

"Do you want my theory?" she says. "Here it is. The children were aware that their father's father had committed suicide and that this fact preyed on their father's mind. Perhaps by a sort of osmosis, it began to prey on theirs too. Things like that are catching."

The rain keeps coming down, dark and heavy against the windows. Barbara watches it. An idea strikes her; she turns back to me.

"Have you ever tried to think a crazy thing?"

I'm puzzled. "I'm not sure. . . ."

"You sit there and try, then stiffen if one comes to you. You try to summon the notion, then block it just as it becomes frightening, interesting."

I think about this for a moment.

"You said all those things about my mother and Helen being brave, taking dares. . . ."

"Yes. The broken bones . . ."

"When exactly did it change?"

"Well. The children grew up. Your grandfather died. I'd say that by the time Harry died it was gone."

"That feeling of invincibility?" I ask.

"Yes . . . ," she says.

"Overcome by a sense of history?"

"Yes, I suppose you could say that," Barbara answers, uncertain. "There were many factors." She looks down into her tea.

I have the guest room under the eaves. The rain drums steady on the roof.

I sit in bed for an hour, reading Hawthorne for American Lit. At eleven I turn off the light.

Lying awake, I repeat the question: "Have you ever tried to think a crazy thing?" There is slight moonlight, and I look up to the unpainted eaves, the dark slope of the wood, and shut my eyes.

The reins are wet, our breath clouds in the morning cold. The horses' sides heave gently, their breathing hard. We reach a moat, shrouded by mist. On the other side is a castle, a Cinderella castle, white with blue turrets. But the horse has planted his feet—we are at the edge of the moat. From high in the saddle I cannot see the bottom—just grey mist, like breath, billowing upward.

I try to remember what dragons breathe . . . fire or smoke? But all I see is soft grey mist.

Grandfather says, "Jump."

134

• • •

It turned out I could not think of something crazy, something odd. All the thoughts that came seemed long familiar. I'd seen the mists rise, I'd seen the moat, I'd seen the horses balk and refuse.

What had become of those rooms now missing? I saw the dark at the top of the stairs, the long lurk of hall, the trail of doors—some open, some shut—I'd seen these too.

I wonder now how I came to know these things, these phantom pictures—bars on the windows, mists rising beyond. But they'd always been there. For a split second it appears perfectly clear: how an idea could creep along the borders of the mind, like a light under a door. How a thought could slip in slyly, like an alligator into a moat. How a notion, dark and quick, could steal into the water and submerge without a sound.

LUNCH
WITH
PEARCE

New York, April 1988

I get the call around eleven o'clock.

"Look, I'm here in the city," says Pearce. "Let's have lunch."

"I can't. I have class in an hour, another at two-thirty."

"Le Relais at one. Looking forward. "

Click.

He's at a table outside. The sunlight's glaring; there's a good breeze. He does not remove his dark glasses as he stands to kiss me hello on the cheek.

The wind whips the edge of the tablecloth as I sit, my back to Madison Avenue. The short sleeves of my dotted navy dress flutter against my arms as Pearce reaches into the ice bucket beside his chair, fills the champagne flute in front of me.

"Nice day," he says.

"I really *do* have a class," I say, watching him pour.

"Of course you do. Where are you at school again?" He knows damn well.

"Columbia."

"Still? That's the one in Harlem, no?"

"Not quite."

"Well . . . it's not Princeton. But then Princeton's not Princeton anymore, either." He pauses. "You'll be staying on at Gran's?"

"I might get my own place. Closer to school."

"Yikes. Stay on at Gran's."

His veal chop arrives. I have a salad.

We finish with lemon tart, crème brûlée, espresso. I know I have to leave for my two-thirty class. I'm feeling slightly drunk, a buzz from the sugar and coffee.

Pearce says, "I had dinner last night with Mum. I told her I was having lunch with you. She said, 'The Bennetts always marry their cousins.' "

"Don't be gross."

"I'm not being gross at all. It's very English."

"Well, that explains a lot."

"What?"

A lot of things, I think. No chins. The Boer War. Bad plumbing. Inbreeding, all . . . "Oh, nothing."

"She *also* said that when Grandaddy was married to Gran, he was fooling around with his cousin Isabel, who later became Lady Wainscott. Now, *that* one even I didn't know."

"Grandfather fooled around?"

"Of course he did. Everyone did then."

137

"Doesn't mean *he* did. Did Gran know about it?"

"Good wives were meant to look the other way. Besides, Gran got more sticking it out than she would have in a settlement. You could buy *great* judges in those days. Nowadays it makes no sense for men to marry. Prenuptials don't hold. You're screwed. I say that if it flies, floats, or fucks, *rent,* don't buy."

"You're gross, Pearce. Did you know that?"

"I'm just realistic. And *you've* got to watch out too, you know."

"What do you mean?"

"Men after your money."

"Well, thank you very much. How extremely kind of you to say—"

"No, not that there won't most likely be a few who think you're cute. Those with more money than you, that is. Any others, you bring them to me, I'll tell you what I think. After all, that was my mother's problem."

"What? Having you tell her how to run her life?"

He doesn't laugh at the joke. "No. Bad men. She chose bad men."

To this I say nothing. Looking satisfied, Pearce clinks his espresso spoon on the saucer and looks up Madison.

———

It's four in the morning. I take his arm as we leave the club. The rain is still coming down, but he doesn't open his umbrella. I clutch at the neck of my short trench.

"Pearce, I'm getting wet."

"Hmm?" *He hands me the umbrella, which I open, holding it over both of us. The dark drops of rain dotting the shoulders of his suit widen slightly as the fabric absorbs them.* "Where do you want to go?" *Pearce asks.*

"Home."

"That's dull." A pause. "What's there?"

"My bed."

"Well. I think I'd like one more drink. Come along?"

"No."

"All right, then."

"Where are you going?" I say.

"Back upstairs."

His eyes flit over me, the little black dress. "Close your coat. You look like a tramp."

"Excuse me?"

A slow cruising cab stops in front of the club.

"That dress. I don't like it. Makes you look like you're for sale."

I look at him but don't say anything as I open the door for myself and climb in. Pearce then hops down to the curb, holding the umbrella high. "So good night," he says, and waits two seconds before closing the door. The cab pulls away, and I can't help but turn and look out through the back window, streaming rain. The floodlight above the club's door shines down on the pavement, a round of sparkling wet glitter. For a moment, Pearce stands in this grimly glowing circle of light, then—hands in his pockets—steps beyond the aureole.

REMEMBERING
HARRY

New York, May 1988

Helen commissioned an Austrian girl, the daughter of someone grand, to make new curtains. The curtains lie across the sofa, a heap of raw silk, yet another shade of cream. Serenna's on the floor, adjusting the new valance box. She sets down her hammer as I come out of the kitchen with two colas and sliced pound cake on a tray.

Serenna takes two nails out of her mouth. She speaks with an Austrian lilt. "I spoke with my Maman on the phone last night, told her about this job because Mrs. Fraser ordered it. Maman says she was once in love with your uncle."

"That would be Harry," I say.

"Yes. Harry Fraser." Serenna takes a sip of cola. "Only she didn't know his last name when she thought she was in love with him. It all sounded so terribly romantic."

"How's that?"

"Ah. Before Maman met my Papa, she and her Maman were visiting in London. Maman was out with friends at a jazz club, and after the show someone introduced her to the piano player. His name was Harry and she thought him wonderfully handsome and he asked her to lunch the next day and she said yes. He said he'd call with the time and place, but that night Maman had stayed out late, then come in smelling of smoke, so the next morning her Maman packed her off to the country to discourage this. So for a while Maman didn't know whether this Harry had rung or how to ring him because he hadn't given his last name, was only 'Harry.' Maman knows all of this now, and who he was, because . . . that lunch the next day? It turned out to be at Wilton's, with her friend Colin Bennett to dine with them."

"Colin Bennett?"

"Yes, he was married to Mrs. Fraser, no?"

"Yes, yes. That's too bad about the mix-up with Harry—"

"Ah, but Maman, she loves this story. At the lunch, your uncle, he took out a pen and drew a picture of her from memory on the back of an ordering ticket. The table was set for three, and he put the picture at the empty place setting. When the waiter arrived he ordered for himself and for Mr. Bennett and then, nodding to the drawing, said, 'Mademoiselle will have the same.' The waiter said something like: 'Is Mademoiselle certain she is hungry?' and your uncle said, 'Yes, Mademoiselle is famished.' Anyway, he made them serve the drawing a complete lunch, pouring wine for her and all."

"Did one of them eat it? Or did the food just sit there?"

"I'm not sure, but it is truly a romantic story. I would have liked to have met your uncle."

I nod.

———

Tales like Serenna's worked their way into my stories for class.

Each week, Professor Thompson photocopied our stories, passed them out to the class of twenty. Everyone liked my first—a period piece about two brothers in a duck blind. But as the semester wore on, there were complaints.

"Your protagonist, isn't this the same guy, just with a different name?"

"Doesn't seem to do much but drink and brood, does he?"

From the end of the discussion table, Professor Thompson pleaded, "I want action. Dialogue. This man *interests* me. I want to see *why* he's so unhappy despite all he's got. I want to see how he thinks, how he interacts."

"I want to see him dead on a highway," grumbled the fat boy who wrote science fiction.

———

There were three people who liked to talk about Harry. Not one of them asked why I wanted to know; at one time everyone wanted to know about Harry.

Linc talked from his Wall Street office, leisurely hanging on the phone during market hours.

Colin talked over drinks at his club one spring afternoon. "I hate New York, but if one *must* cross the great puddle, there is at least this place," he said, giving a sweeping hand gesture to the silent open space, the rows of old books and tall windows.

Barbara Prewitt had of course told me stories before. This time she wrote a long letter, typed single space. She asked me to forgive her for not writing by hand, but she liked to type. "I typed all your mother's papers at Radcliffe in exchange for her editing mine. She could never learn to type; I could never learn to spell."

——

From Barbara's letter, spelled correctly:

Harry was so glamorous. He was older than your mother and I by almost seven years, so we never spent much time with him.

It was in the third grade your mother and I became close. The first time I met Harry was the following Easter, down at Heyton Hall. He came down from school just for the weekend, brought lots of presents—those hollow sugar Easter eggs with white fancy trim and a peephole to the panorama inside. I remember being surprised and touched that he brought one for me. I agreed with your mother; he was completely thoughtful and charming, just the kind of man to marry when we grew up. ("After vet school," your mother would add. "Marriage is out until after I finish vet school.")

Linc told us jokes. He was closer to our age, less remote. And he was home more often—he'd have a tutor at Broadhurst to finish out the year after leaving school somewhere. I think it embarrassed him, getting kicked out because of grades. When Harry got kicked out, it was for something clever or daring. But it was great fun having Linc at Broadhurst all those weekends. He rewired the Redbugs—these 1930s go-carts with red seats, wooden floor slats, and hooded headlights. We'd race them all round. He also told us dirty jokes, then turned all red and flustered when we asked him to explain.

143

You have to remember about your uncle Linc—he was not an intellectual. He was also the butt of a lot of the family humor. Linc was good at motor things, good with his hands in a family good with their mouths. Your Gran, Helen, and Harry were all talkers. When your mother and I were finally old enough to join the adults at dinner, we found that their games were charades, ghost, and twenty questions, just as ours had been when we ate in the kitchen.

Colin, on his second drink:

After Linc was tossed out of Westminster, his father took him to Alaska for two weeks of hunting. They did have that in common—guns and game. Linc treasured that trip with his father.

Harry could shoot—was a fair shot, in fact—but his sport was tennis. Social. More women around. And he looked quite gallant all in white, leaping over nets. A graceful man, your uncle.

Besides shooting, Linc had a mind for mechanics. Not that that was worth anything to someone in his position. But he kept at it, fiddling with the engines of the older cars in the garage at Broadhurst. That's how he and Darcy got to be so close. I don't suppose you ever knew Darcy. Was your grandfather's chauffeur, fine fellow. Had Linc learning more about engines than the rest of us thought he'd ever learn about anything.

Linc, on office time:

I was dyslexic, you know, long before they knew what it was or how to recognize it. The schools and everyone else just thought I was slow, and for a while there I believed them. Anyway, I had to defend myself a lot. Darcy was the one who taught me to fight. I came back from

Westminster on a long weekend and said, "Darcy, you're Irish—will you show me how to fight?" He said first that I shouldn't be fighting, that I should learn to handle things by talking them out the way gentlemen do, but then the next day he brought me a set of brass knuckles and taught me how to use them. "Not for that school of yours, you hear," he told me. "But just so you know." After that, we'd box behind the garage whenever I'd come home. He got me to where I was pretty good. Darcy was like a father to me, you know.

Something occurs to Colin. He stabs his finger in the air:

Now, your mother, Sarah, she was the serious one. I remember one morning at Broadhurst . . . Linc had read somewhere, don't know where—funny, actually, that he'd come up with this, because we doubted he read his science books or much of anything else, for that matter— well, he did read somewhere that if one placed dry ice in an airtight container, the pressure would build up and cause the whole thing to explode. Well, your uncle Linc thought this was a fine idea. Went out to the garage and asked Darcy where he could get hold of some of this dry ice stuff. Course Darcy, being a sensible fellow, asked what he wanted it for.

"Why, to make an explosion," said Linc. Well, for once Darcy put his foot down.

Your grandfather was at Broadhurst that weekend. Driving back from the stables before lunch, he asked Darcy how the boys were, and Darcy told him what Linc had requested.

"Dry ice? But why?" asked your grandfather.

"To make an explosion."

"Oh? But how?"

Next thing you know, Darcy's been sent to town, and

God knows where he found the stuff, but there he was, two hours later, with a box of dry ice and ten jars from the kitchen. Your grandfather and Linc lined the jars on the edge of the west terrace, past the fountain. Your grandfather sent up for the rest of us children and we came and gathered round as he dropped a chunk in a jar, screwed down the lid, then walked away backward, shooing us further behind. True to the book, the jar exploded. Linc was delighted. The two continued like this, making explosions until they ran out of ice or jars—I don't remember which.

Your mother had left after just the first jar. She'd gone back to the kitchen, where she was making a doggy cake for Bobo's birthday. Candles and everything. She was no fun at all.

From Barbara's letter:

William Fraser expected his children to grow up with spirit, but he did not dictate their choices. They could have turned out as either card-carrying Communists or McCarthyites—it would have been fine by him, as long as they could back their choices with strong arguments. He had found his own philosophy in his thirties, after a long, hard search. Maybe he didn't know how to dictate, since he hadn't had a father around to guide him past the age of twelve. He was wonderful with all of us children, but when he did spend time it seemed as if it were Christmas and he were Santa Claus, someone not to expect more than once a year.

But by the time your mother and I started at Radcliffe, he was an old man. Then just when his children reached the age where they seek advice, he died.

Things seem slow at Linc's office. When I ask if I'm keeping him, he says no, no, and continues:

146

You know, I used to worry a lot when I was your age. This story's from when I was at Hazelden, drying out. God, I was a mess. Your uncle Harry came once to visit me and listen to me wonder if I was going to get well, and he looked around and said something like this:

"You know, Lincoln, it doesn't do any good to worry about these things, because one way or another they're going to solve themselves. You think you've got to know now whether you're going to be happy in twenty years, but you just can't know. And it's not going to help to worry, never has.

"Remember," Harry said to me then, "remember when you were six or so and I told you that there was no such thing as Father Christmas? Well, that was very wrong of me to do, but anyway . . . It wouldn't have bothered you as much if I could prove for sure there wasn't one. But you wanted the truth one way or another, because what if you grew up never being sure . . . And then you'd have kids, and what would you do? Would you buy them presents or count on Father Christmas? Would you sneak downstairs before your kids were awake, and if Father Christmas hadn't come, then you'd put these backup presents you've got hidden in a closet under the tree?"

He told me I was a worrier. All those logistics, struggling with all that extra brainwork when I didn't have to. He said, "Now do you see? Problems have a way of solving themselves."

When I repeat this story to Colin he looks surprised:

Oh, they both had problems. But Harry could conceal them. Linc wasn't smart enough. Or maybe Linc was smarter than we knew.

Harry traveled a lot those five or so years after school. Lots of parties, lots of girls.

He liked art, art objects. Blew a lot of money at La Vieille Russie. Got some beautiful things, though. Wrought gold and enamel—boxes, eggs. Fabergé mostly. Then he'd help his friends choose things, for a while called himself an art consultant. It gave him something respectable to talk about. But then all of a sudden he just wanted to play the piano. Suddenly, everything was jazz. . . .

More than anything else, Harry wanted to be Ray Charles. Maybe the only thing he wanted. Maybe the first.

Linc is sounding weary. I hear footsteps in his office, the sound of paper sliding onto his desk. He thanks his secretary, continues:

It was The Castle. The players at The Castle. If it weren't for them . . . No. I don't know.

But he had some good times there. Was playing well for a time. He never got to actually play The Castle, but he did hang out with those who did when they'd warm up in the afternoons, or play late, after the crowds were gone.

It was your grandfather who first took him there. Father knew he was sick, wanted to squeeze in a lot of things at the end. I was at Hazelden then. I'd checked myself in, you know.

But those players at The Castle—the old blacks, the good ones—they told Harry that he'd never get good unless he smoked dope. "White boy, you ain't felt nothin'," and they were probably right. So he smoked. And it worked at first. And then came the rest of it. There was the heroin, and he was an addict.

Before, his piano had had this mechanical quality. He'd be right on the notes, but it would sound like he was one step behind.

So with the drugs he was looser, but he still wasn't reaching it. I could have told him the drugs weren't going to do it for him. Hell, I knew that. More was slipping away than was coming to him. He still wanted it all to come to him.

"I think," Linc finishes, "that when he finally did it . . . he meant it."

———

So he died of an overdose . . . I don't know how I got it into my head that there had been a gun.

"I suppose to shoot yourself takes a lot of courage," says Linc about Great-Grandfather.

> Stops and beaters oft unseen
> Lurk behind some leafy screen . . .
> FOLLOW NOT ACROSS THE LINE.

PART III

SUMMER
GAMES II

Maine, August 1988

"Oh, God!"

"Just run in!"

I'm inching into the water, numb to my knees. I clutch the towel still wrapped tight around my shoulders. Felicity's doing her morning strokes lengthwise across the inlet. The sea is icy cold.

From behind I hear quick footsteps kicking up pebbles and then long splashes as Beverly Anne enters the water. When she passes me the water cuts her stride, she screams and plunges, and—except for a wavy yellow view of her swimsuit—disappears.

Beverly Anne surfaces, doing the backstroke. She yells

to Felicity, who floats further out: "So if God meant me to be a polar bear, where's my white fur coat?!"

"Cold storage!?" Felicity rebuts. She and Beverly Anne like each other enormously, which I find surprising. Felicity being so serious and Beverly Anne so . . . Texan.

But then again, Beverly Anne is the straightforward type of Texas girl. Even though she may arrive with a full set of electric Clairol Kindness rollers in their own Fendi tote, she would never shy from dunking her head in the sea. Plus she has a job with the Texas zoological society. This scores big with Felicity, who said: "I can't fathom what she sees in Pearce, but some mysteries *are* beyond us."

We shake off streams of water, rubbing hard with towels until the feeling, tingling warm, comes back to our fingers and toes. The air—once cold—seems fine now, the pebbles soft and dry under our feet. Felicity, her face beaded with water, asks, "That wasn't so bad, was it?" She blots her face quickly with a blue towel, grabs the length of her hair, and starts to wring out water.

A terrific yawn from the porch, and we look up to see it's Lulu. Lulu rubs her eyes in vigorous pantomime. (She is—did I not mention?—an actress/model.) Lulu is wearing nothing but panties and a pink shirt—Pearce's tab-collared broadcloth, barely buttoned.

"Goodness, last night I didn't think you all were really going to get up to swim. . . . I mean, I thought you were *joking*."

"Nope. Not joking," says Felicity, pressing the towel to her ear, shaking out water.

Beverly Anne calls, "The ocean's super. You should give it a try."

"Maybe." Lulu's doing stretches, arching backward, hands on her hips. Then, lazily, a few windmill toe touches, crossing over once to each side.

"Was it wet?" she asks, straightening up.

Lulu goes everywhere Pearce goes, except when Pearce vanishes ("for, like, no reason at all"). When this happens, Lulu must track him down at the Ritz, where he'll be with another woman, and then the rest of us must read about it on "Page Six."

Despite Lulu's presence this morning, Pearce swears she was not expressly invited to Maine. "It's like with suits," he explained. "A white linen suit might be fine for Buenos Aires, but you sure aren't going to wear it to the Links Club." It was Beverly Anne whom Pearce had asked up—"Not that she floats my boat anymore, but she is fun."

Beverly Anne is several years older than Pearce. Five years, actually. One would never know it from looking at her.

Lulu is Pearce's age but has been around for seemingly forever. "Shopworn" is the verdict from Felicity. In the seven years Lulu's been in New York, she's made such enemies that when I finally met her I was taken aback by how well she looked. Lulu's all long apricot-colored hair (worn with little-girl ribbons and clips) and long legs. ("Wrapped them around every busboy in New York," one of her friends told me, in confidence.)

Lulu has pale freckled skin and bone-thin limbs. This morning her toenails—polished and curling onto the fog-gray deck paint of the porch—gleam coral.

"Listen," Lulu says to Felicity. "Do you know where the tea's kept? There's, like, absolutely no one in the kitchen."

"The pantry. Third shelf down."

"Thanks. You're a love." She sweeps back inside, shirttail billowing over the sticks of her legs.

I sit on the little chair beside the bed as Felicity drags her duffel from the closet. She's going back to Connecticut a few days early.

Guinness lies on the wooden floor, his ruff flat, his coat clean and glossy. Felicity brushed him out by the garage yesterday afternoon. Pearce drove up to find a cloud of silvery hairs floating in the chilly sunlight, causing him to sneeze and prompting Lulu to gape and coo, "Ooh—pretty!"

Jeans, an armload of sweatshirts, and Felicity's packed.

"Can I drive you to the airstrip?" I ask.

"I certainly hope so."

Minutes later we're on the front porch, everyone saying goodbye, except for Pearce, who plays tennis in the mornings. Stella comes out and tells Felicity to give Helen her best.

"She really is the dearest person I know. I pray for her and you."

Guinness jumps into the back seat of the station wagon.

The airstrip is on the other side of the island. Felicity talks as I drive.

"It'll be good to get back to work. I hate having other people look after the beasties."

This is what Felicity says, but she's also leaving early to see her mother. Last month Helen was, as Linc put it, "carted off."

"She jumped out of a window this time," Linc said. "But only from two stories up."

Felicity nixed Silver Hill and found another hospital—a "we-mean-business hospital," Felicity called it, an hour from the stables. Today is the first day that Felicity will be able to visit. Helen's doctor requested that she have no visitors for a while, suggested that seeing her children would be counterproductive to treatment.

We worry, of course, how Pearce is coping. So far he comments freely on the hospitalization. "Of course I agree it's a good idea for Mum to see someone about this killing-herself thing," he said. "But Felicity's gone and had her penned in a loony bin."

We spot the Cessna's descent just as we turn off the main road. We park as it lands, turning, taxiing back up the runway. The wind from the propellers bows the heads of Queen Anne's lace that fringe the strip. They bob until the engine's cut.

"He's going too?" I say, nodding to Guinness.

"Yup."

A short one-armed hug as Felicity pulls her duffel from the station wagon.

"Good luck," I say.

"You too."

Pearce's tennis match ends after she's left.

At dinner that night Pearce tells the remaining guests that tomorrow we must be up by nine or die—"missing the dog show's not an option." After dinner there's a tray of chilled liqueurs to pour into thin crystal balloons with short stems, then the Lowes come over, and in the morning it's a very sorry lot that drags itself out to the station wagon.

Beverly Anne, beside me in the back seat, wears lavender silk Bermudas and has her hands folded over a straw clutch.

Lulu swings her legs around into the front passenger seat. She's in tennis shorts and holds Fala on her lap, stroking the Lhasa's head. "Pearce, do you have any pretty ribbon?" Lulu asks. "We could make Sweetie here a bow."

Pearce turns to survey.

"Where's Guinness?"

"Connecticut," Beverly Anne answers sweetly.

"What?" asks Pearce after a pause, his voice low.

Pearce drives angrily, slapping the steering wheel. "It's *just* like Felicity to make off with him like that!" Lulu reaches over to stroke his hair, but he bats her hand away.

Beverly Anne, gazing out the window, smiles serenely.

Pearce continues to mutter under his breath.

"Isn't Guinness Aunt Helen's?" I say. "Felicity probably took him so that your mother could see him—"

"That would be all very *well and good*," Pearce replies, biting down on every word. "Except that Felicity knows *damn well* that Mum doesn't *want* to see him. Our mother, you see, has gotten it into her head that Guinness is a *wolf*. At last count, Mum couldn't *stand* to even have him in the *house*. See what this doctor thing of Felicity's has done? *Damn it!*" He slams the heel of his hand against the steering wheel. "I swear she just does these things to *provoke* me."

The event is on Grace Atcheson's lawn. We arrive late.

The small nonsporting dog class tours the ring. Three-year-old Annabelle Lowe, who was to show Fala, is being pulled around by another family's Pomeranian.

"Good God, *now* what do we do?" Pearce scans the

crowd of children sitting on the grass around the roped-
off ring. The sun glints off the bay, and Pearce shades his
eyes with the hand holding the leash. "The key to this
contest is a cute kid. . . ."

"How about that one?" Beverly Anne points to a little
girl with curly hair, who's just risen. Dew has wet the back
of her blue checked jumper.

"That's the Granger's girl. Don't know them."

"Pearce, I'll show him," says Lulu.

"You're too *old*," Pearce snaps.

Down in the ring, the judges break from their huddle.
One confers with Mr. Morris, the club president, with
slicked hair and megaphone. Mr. Morris awards a Scottie
the white fourth-place ribbon.

"Too late," grumbles Pearce.

It's all for charity—the Island Historical Society.

Young mothers stand together in clumps. They wear
snug cotton sweaters with turned-down polo collars. Most
wear Tretorns, a few are in scuffed Dr. Scholl's, left over
from the seventies. They have straight hair, hard edges
hanging just above their shoulders.

Their younger daughters sit in a row just beyond the
ring; a row of backs in Laura Ashley jumpers. You can
see the side of their faces when they turn to whisper
or giggle, their hair just brushed, scraped back with
grosgrain-covered barrettes.

The older daughters, of boarding school or college age,
sit farther away, sprawled on the little hill, dressed in tie
dye, men's cotton shorts, no shoes. They have long straggly
hair and houseguests that worry their mothers.

The prettiest in the row of younger girls is the Barton
girl, about nine, deeply tanned, with a blond braid. The
shorter hairs on the back of her neck have escaped the

plait, and in a very pretty gesture she reaches back with both small hands to smooth them flat. "Wait six years," says Billy Lowe to Pearce, and they nod and laugh conspiratorially.

After the Pomeranian wins the blue, Annabelle Lowe drops the leash and scampers up the hill to her father.

Amanda Lowe follows. Pearce calls to her. "You would not *believe* what my sister's done now."

Lulu, bent over in her brief white shorts, talks baby talk to a wandering toddler. Behind her, two small boys whisper that the lady isn't wearing underwear.

After dinner that night Pearce excuses himself, returns in five minutes changed into jeans and a red sweater, claps his hands, and announces "Kiddie party. Get in the car."

The party is at the Matthewses' tonight; their parents are off-island. The lights are bright, but there's a bear rug, cases of Moosehead, bootleg tapes of the Dead, the Stones, REM. About twenty kids are in the room, some of them dancing. The long-haired Matthews boy, head bobbing like a rag doll, hops around to "Sugar Magnolia" with someone's au pair—a dark-haired Belgian girl who wears her jeans cut off and cuffed at the knee, white Keds on her feet.

Lulu, looking around, takes hold of Pearce's arm. "Pearce, there are twelve-year-olds here. . . ."

"Good. Just your speed, right?"

Gordon Emerson drives Beverly Anne and me back. The three of us sit at the edge of the porch with cans of Fresca, talking. Soon Beverly Anne goes to bed.

Suddenly, there's a loud burst on the porch beside us.

I jump up. "What was that!"

Another, then sounds of giggling from the window above.

"Pearce!" I groan, turning around.

"Goddamn, they're *eggs*," says Gordon, getting up, wiping his khakis. He turns to look up at the window. "He's in that one, ducking down."

I call, "Pearce, I know you're home!"

Pearce's head pops up. "Ah-hah! Had to come home! To see if my dear cousin was carrying on with undesirables! But now I see it's only Gordon. Hullo, Gordon!"

Another head pops up in the window. It's the Belgian au pair girl, the source of the giggles. "Alo, Gordon!"

"Good evening."

"So what's going on?" says Pearce.

"Not much," I say. "Where's Lulu?"

"How should I know? Billy'll give her a ride. So to speak. Where's Bev Anne?"

"Gone to bed."

"Good for her. Who with?"

"I won't even stoop to answer that question." I turn away.

"Let's wake her. Egg carton ready?" The au pair nods. "No, wait. We'll get some warm water or something. You guys coming?"

Moments later, a foghorn blast and screams crash down from above. Billy, carrying a bottle of Moët, walks onto the porch.

"I hear the games have begun. Think you should warn your esteemed host that I've brought his girlfriend back. I'm too old for this."

"Where *is* Lulu?" I ask.

"I left her in the kitchen, making a marshmallow fluff and potato chip sandwich. I couldn't bear to watch."

· · ·

The lights go on up in Beverly Anne's room. We hear several sets of running footsteps, doors slamming.

"So who is that Wascally Wabbit torturing now?" asks Billy.

"His *other* girlfriend," I say.

"Ooh—Texas tea. And us with the best seats in the house."

Gordon asks Billy if the Matthewses' party is over.

"Naw; slowed down some. I got bored. I think I'm getting too old for that stuff. In my day people would take drugs, sit around and talk. Now they take drugs, sit around, and talk about the fact they just took drugs."

Another door slams. Beverly Anne's light goes out. There's a shout and a loud thud from upstairs.

Lulu walks out onto the porch licking one finger, a gooey sandwich on a plate. "Hello. Gordon. Meredith. *Love* the peace and quiet here on your little island." She eats half the sandwich, then announces she's going to bed. "And for the record, please tell Master Pearce that I went *alone.*"

Pearce walks out a few minutes later, the au pair girl skulking behind him.

"Billy! Always a pleasure."

Billy gets up, and they shake hands with mock formality. "Good evening, Pearce. Real white of you to have us. I hear you're being naughty."

"Prank night!"

"Oh, Jesus. And me without the wife. How she'll hate to miss it." Billy shakes his head mournfully.

"Getting smart now, are we, Billy? Want to go in the pool again?"

"You have *never* thrown me in the pool."

"Have so."

Billy hands Pearce the bottle.

"Swigging direct, I see," says Pearce, taking it. "You're turning into an old bum, Billy." Pearce takes a sip and swallows. "You shouldn't drink this cheap stuff. It interferes with quality drugs." Then, surveying us, he claps his hands. "*So!*" We gaze back at him. "Look, Billy—we have Gordon and Meredith and this dear girl tonight." He nods at the au pair, who just giggles. "Who's first—the sleepers or the neighbors?"

An hour later the five of us are in the basement laundry. There is a low, odd hum from the overhead light, flickering unsteadily. Socks and polo shirts dry on a rack. Billy swats at a long curling fly strip, darkly speckled.

Pearce hauls a large box of Tide from the utility shelf.

"God, this is heavy. Someone ought to write the company, tell them to make smaller boxes." He grunts under the weight.

"They do," says Billy.

"So this is what they call 'economy-sized'? What's Stella trying to do, save us money?"

"I'd suggest," starts Billy, "*if* I were participating in this idiocy, transferring the detergent into smaller sacks."

"Good thinking, Billy."

Gordon announces he's going home. As I walk him out, we see the sign Lulu has pinned to the door. Crayoned in fiery lipstick: "HOTEL HELL. Check in: 6 P.M. Check out: NEVER."

"Are the Wingates ever going to have a surprise for their morning swim!" Pearce gloats, filling plastic bags with detergent.

"Is this in retaliation for anything in particular?" asks Billy.

Pearce considers. "Pure malice."

"Well, fine."

"Commandos ready?"

Billy and I follow only as far as the pricker bushes, the wooded line that marks the property. Pearce, oblivious to thorns, plows through. The au pair trails, issuing small whimpers of complaint.

The end of the night usually finds Pearce in the kitchen—making omelets, noise, a mess—with the tennis pro, people's staff, hangers-on. Or, other nights, he'll slip in quietly, picking up bottles of Moët, a car engine running outside, someone waiting.

But tonight he's still not back. Beverly Anne and I sit on the kitchen counter, a pint of Ben & Jerry's Mint Oreo between us, two spoons.

Beverly Anne's got her quilted robe over her nightgown. "Trying to sleep on prank night is like waiting for the other shoe to drop."

Beverly Anne talks about the summer Pearce stayed with her in Texas.

"You wouldn't think this, what with the way he's been acting, but Pearce is actually a jealous, one-woman type. Summer after his sophomore year, he was staying with me in Fort Worth, and I get home from work one evening and see these two dozen yellow roses on the hall table. Beside them there's this neat little pile of shreds— what used to be the card. Turned out they were from Kip Agar, who's this divine boy from Midland who'd got my birthday wrong, but Pearce just ranted and raved, went into a snit for days. . . ."

"Sounds awful."

"Oh, hell, Pearce and I'd have fun, though. We'd just sit around the floor in our underwear, drinking champagne. We'd sit there and laugh about the lengths other girls would go to track him down."

"Really?"

"And you know how Pearce and your aunt are. They depend a lot on each other. It got so sad when she'd call us in the middle of the night. 'I'm so happy you've found each other,' she'd be saying. 'I wish I had someone like you two have each other.' I know this family stuff is personal, and I wouldn't bring this up if it weren't for his mom's new problems and all. . . . I just thought you should know, since you're so close to Pearce."

"Thank you . . . But actually, we're not that close."

"He thinks you are." A pause. "So I guess that's somethin' you should know."

I ask Beverly Anne why she puts up with Lulu.

"The thing with Pearce," Beverly Anne says, "is that he needs a yes-girl and a no-girl." She shrugs, not sadly. "I became the no-girl at the end of that summer, when he wanted to leave Princeton, stay in Texas. I kicked him out, told him to write his thesis, finish his degree. He finally went back east—accusations flying: 'You don't love me!' So Lulu's the yes-girl; I'm the no-girl."

There are light footsteps from the hall, and there's Lulu, clutching at the neck of a terry robe. She glances at us, her face pinched, nervous.

"Want some ice cream, honey?" says Beverly Anne.

Lulu looks at us, shakes her head, and wanders out.

Beverly Anne, taking another spoonful, lets it rest and melt in her mouth. Then says, serenely, "Lulu's looking for Pearce."

And indeed, there is still no sign of him.

• • •

Noon the next day, the sun is hot. Stella wants to know how many for lunch—and have I seen Pearce?

He turns up at twelve-thirty with the Lowes. He's mumbling, preoccupied, antsy. He shuffles around, rubbing his face with his hand like a dog cleaning its muzzle.

Lunch on the porch, much clinking of glasses. Afterward Stilton and pears.

"Stilton! What, no port?" asks Billy, joking.

Pearce says, "Might have some. But you'd have to earn it."

"Say the word," Billy dares.

"Let's have a dirty story, Billy."

The story's told. Beverly Anne and Amanda laugh along, I smile politely, Lulu puts on that she's offended.

"Bring on the port!" shouts Billy.

Pearce taps me on the shoulder, I follow him into the kitchen. As he pulls the port glasses from a cabinet, he tells me, delightedly, just what happened last night.

It was, of course, the little Belgian girl.

". . . So there we are in the Wingates' Whaler. We're drifting, bottles of champagne—"

"From where?"

"My car. Don't interrupt. Bottles piling up in the bottom of the Whaler, and this girl just *doesn't* stop. It gets to be dawn, and she wants to paddle ashore, so I throw the paddles overboard and she says, 'What about the motor?' but she *believes* me when I say it doesn't work— of course I'm stepping on the fuel line—so we crash out there until we float by Billy's, where they're having coffee on the deck. So I switch on the motor and wave, putter

166

over, and yell, 'Have you got Bloodies and a bed?!' So there we are, feeling like hell, about to sit and have a nice breakfast with Billy and Amanda, but then this stupid girl insists that she's got to go back to the Ingrams' right then to make breakfast for their beastly children."

We return to the table with the port and new glasses.

Beverly Anne excuses herself. "I hear men like to be alone with their port and cigars."

"Oh? You got some cigars around here?" says Billy.

Upstairs, Beverly Anne takes her flowered toilet kit and Clairol rollers from the bathroom.

"Are you packing?" I ask.

"When they're this way, that's what one does."

"What. Is this because of Lulu . . . ?"

"Naw; he just doesn't need me when he's like this. I came thinking I might help. It's like at kindergarten. The more a little boy needs his mama, the more he doesn't like to show it. But I've had it for now. Look out for him, will you?"

That night I catch hell from Pearce.

"You should have come and told me *immediately* that she was leaving. The charter company knows me. I could have gotten her fogged in."

I point out that the day was sunny.

"Maybe not in Bangor. She was making a connection in Bangor. How would she have known it wasn't foggy in *Bangor?* She would still be here if you—"

"Pearce, she would have taken the ferry."

"Meredith, she would not—" His eyes are shut.

"Pearce, she would have *swam.*"

• • •

Pearce stays mad, certain I'd told Beverly Anne about the au pair.

Lulu does learn of the au pair but stays.

Felicity telephones to say she's seen Helen. Pearce is out when she calls.

He spends the rest of August on the tennis court, breaking two racquets before switching to graphite.

WALK-IN-HAND

Connecticut, September 1988

Saturday. I take a cab from the station to the stables.

It's hot for September, dusty. Felicity's in the ring, doing a walk-in-hand: leading the horse, restraining him when he tries to rear, readying him for saddle training. Felicity's dirty grey breeches are wet with grit, and her sleeveless button-down bares her arms, tan and strong as a man's.

Further down the fence there's a guy with a crew cut and a grey sweatshirt, watching her too. He waves to me, then walks up, fingers hooked over jeans pockets.

"You're Meredith, I guess," he says, friendly. "I'm Hugh." He extends his hand.

We talk, and I remember Pearce mentioning him last spring. "Felicity's got a boyfriend, finally," Pearce said, "and of course he's completely awful. Wears one of those big computerized watches that tells you the rainfall in Tibet—you know, sort of mission command."

Hugh played ball in college a few years ago, might have gone pro until he messed up his knee. Now he teaches high school math, coaches swimming. I picture a silver whistle around his neck.

I find Hugh completely nice. And in the stable office, when I say this to Felicity, she replies, "Yes, he is, isn't he?" And not another word.

Felicity must be back to give a lesson in an hour, so the three of us will lunch at her place.

Felicity drives us down a gravel road from the stable, a road flanked by stretches of dirt, patchy weeds, and aluminum fencing. Her apartment is on the second floor, off the back entrance of a dirty white frame house. A telephone pole with electric wires stands a little ways from the unpainted stairway built onto the back. There's a dog in the yard—part yellow Lab, fat, chained to a post. He thumps his tail on the dirt when he sees the truck pull up.

"Poor Frito," says Felicity. She bends down, and Frito offers his head for a pat, slurps his tongue around her hand, and sniffs. "They're beasts, his owners. But they let me take him to the stables on weekends when they're home. They think he's here as some sort of watchdog when they're not. Funny, chaining a watchdog. Hard to get a good chunk out of a robber when you're all tied up. Not that you'd take a chunk out of anyone, would you, boy? No, you're a lover, not a fighter."

Felicity undoes the chain, and Frito bounds up the

stairs ahead of us, turns and waits on the landing, four paws skittering in excitement.

Inside, Felicity scoots behind a screen that hides the kitchenette. "It'll just be a minute." Hugh and I sit on the sofa and talk above the slam of pots and cabinet doors.

He points out an Ansel Adams sort of poster, framed, of a snow-capped mountain.

"I got her that, since she didn't have anything on the walls when I met her. It's of Mount Rainier. I've been trying to get her to come out to Washington, maybe go camping. It's beautiful any time of year. If you don't mind rain."

"*I don't!*" yells Felicity from behind the kitchen screen. "Just find me the two free days, and I'm there."

"She's been saying that for a year," says Hugh. "But she prefers the beasties to me." Hugh says this jokingly, sort of kidding.

The other walls in the studio are bare. The furniture looks as if it came with the place, vinyl leatherette. One window, short red curtains half drawn, lets in light. The carpet is beige, well vacuumed, save for near the door, where clumps of dried mud lie tracked around the boot pull.

"Lunch is served," Felicity calls, carrying out forks and napkins, paper plates of beef macaroni casserole.

"Smells great," Hugh says.

"I made this last night; just had to reheat it." Plates on our laps, we begin.

"It's good, as usual," says Hugh.

"Recipe's from *Family Circle*, thank you very much. I read it in line at the supermarket."

"This really is good," I say, for some reason moved.

"There's dessert too."

Hugh looks up. "Whoa, do my ears deceive me?"

171

"Fruited Jell-O with Cool Whip," Felicity replies.

"My domestic goddess."

"Don't get used to it."

After lunch, Hugh drives me to the station in the truck.

"Felicity's been real busy today. I know she's sorry she couldn't spend more time with you. She's been trying to get all eight horses in before driving to Stamford."

"Stamford? You mean to the hospital?"

"Just about every day now."

"She didn't say so."

"Calls in at noon. Some days they'll say she can see her, some days no. But seems it's been a good week. That's why she's a bit behind at work."

"Huh." I'd been told that Helen hadn't wanted visitors. I'd accepted that news gladly. Guiltily, I ask Hugh, "How is Felicity when she gets back from there?"

"The same. Herself."

"That's good."

Hugh is silent. It feels strange talking about Felicity behind her back.

"Felicity certainly does do a lot," I say, awkwardly.

"Yeah. She's something, isn't she?" He does not seem happy when he says this.

We've reached the station, and I thank Hugh for the ride.

——

Years ago at Heyton Hall, Chessy had her poodle. When Felicity and Pearce were children, they'd be served their dinner on trays in Chessy's small sitting room off the kitchen, eating by the light of the TV and a bubble-glass lamp.

They'd eat at seven, before the adults. The Newlywed

Game came on then, and Chessy would watch in her slippers, the poodle lying across her foot.

Felicity was puzzled by the show, cynical about marriage, the notions of trust and dependence. "Mum should go on that show," Felicity once said to Chessy. "She's constantly a newlywed."

She would say things like this, but then she would watch Chessy's poodle as he lay sleeping across the foot of his mistress, like an anchor. And she'd wonder.

LUNCH
AGAIN

New York, September 1988

Pearce is in town "just for the day."
We meet at Le Relais at one. The bright weather persists.

Pearce nods to my menu. "The veal chop's good."

"I think I'll have a salad." Pause. "I saw Felicity last week. She's doing well."

Pearce shrugs. "Good for her."

"She goes to the hospital just about every day."

"That would explain why Mama's still in the bin." Pause. "Have you met the awful boyfriend?"

"Felicity's?"

"*Yes,* Felicity's."

"Hugh?"

"I think that's his name."

"I liked him."

Pearce gives a faint groan and shakes his head. Listlessly, he slumps in his chair, rumpling his suit jacket. There are dark circles under his eyes.

"So you're going to London for how long?" I ask.

"A few days."

"Then you'll be back?"

"Paris."

"Oh."

"Then Italy."

His veal chop arrives. I eat my salad.

———

Remember that Pearce is named for Harry.

When Henry Pearce and Felicity were six and eight, they lived in Paris. Helen would take Pearce with her to dress fittings—Saint Laurent, Givenchy. Pearce would sit nicely on high spindly chairs just outside the dressing room, the tops of his feet touching the floor as ladies in grey would bring him plates of thin chicken and watercress sandwiches, the crusts trimmed to nothingness. Helen would come out in a dress, and Pearce would turn and clap his hands and say, "The red, Mother, get the red!"

And she would.

THROUGH
THE WOODS

**South Carolina, Thanksgiving
Day, 1988**

>   . . . In the morning I walk under col-
> onnades of live oak, each trunk rising dark and thick from
> the vivid carpet of ryegrass. The branches drip with Span-
> ish moss, grey-green clumps, arching over the grass. Spots
> of sunlight burst through onto the yellow-green lawn,
> each new blade stretching up with all its might to meet
> it.

———

There is no blessing.

We have local oysters to start, then dove, quail, pureed
sweet potatoes. "Sure feel sorry for the poor suckers

eating turkey," says Linc, the only reference to the holiday.

Gilbert brings out a pumpkin pie, cuts big slices, since we're just the four of us. Felicity says, "Make a wish," as we angle our forks to the tip.

After lunch Gran takes the golf cart for a spin around the gardens. Felicity and I ride along, me standing in back, both of us clutching the rails as Gran guns the pedal and bounces us onward with no regard for bumps or tree roots rising and twisting across her path.

We return as Willy pulls into the turnaround with the dogcart (a green wooden trailer hooked behind a Ford). He greets Linc in his usual manner, motioning down toward Bonnie.

"That ain't no hunting dog, Mr. Linc. That a house pet."

The spaniel wags her tail. Bonnie goes everywhere Linc goes. The two of them will troop into Gran's cream living room, tracking mud. Gilbert despairs, but Gran, having never cleaned a carpet in her life, notices not. Willy and Linc drive off.

Sometimes at Heyton Hall it gets so that I can barely dress myself. In those hours after lunch my limbs will feel heavy and I'll lie in the chaise longue in my room, unable even to read. Warm sunlight streams onto the carpet, and in the magnolia tree outside the birds are quiet. It feels as if our whole world's napping. Then at four-thirty I'll haul myself downstairs for tea (raisin toast and silver pots heavy on a butler's tray). Gran pours, then sits with her reading glasses and Agatha Christie, waiting for the afternoon hunters to return.

But today Felicity pulls me from my slump, dragging me out for a ride.

The men at the stables used to bring horses saddled to the door, but Felicity won't have this. "Otherwise, around here, we'd just go from sitting position to sitting position."

The stables are a short walk down the plantation's main road. Behind the front paddock, twelve stalls stretch beneath a white frame cupola, tack rooms at either end.

Quail chicks, tiny and perfect, with soft downy spots, race back and forth in their pens with each new crunch of gravel from foot or tractor.

Bits of hay and dust spin in the sunlight. Heads poke out of the stalls in a sweet line. These horses are not grand; they are shooting ponies—thick creatures with broad backs and some age, indifferent to gunfire.

A groom pours a cup of oats into each trough. Satisfied tails swish at the rear, chasing the flies from side to side, the oats disappearing with the dry dusty wiffling of nostrils.

Felicity, who thinks of these things, takes a peeled carrot from her mac pocket, snaps it in two, then with hand flat offers one half to Belle. She slips me the other half.

"Feed it to the mule. I always feel sorry for mules."

"Why's that?" Ears back, grey lips long, the big animal blows hot on my hand as he seizes the carrot.

She shrugs. "Because they can't reproduce."

"Oh, right."

"But then again, maybe that's not so bad." She pats Belle. "What about you?" she asks. "Are you going to be brave?" She means have a family.

"What, buck our odds?"

"Yes. Exactly."

"I don't know."

"I don't, either."

A moment later, tightening the girth, Felicity says, harshly, as if we're arguing, "Whatever Pearce or my mother will tell you, it's *not* in the blood."

We pass through Middle Woods at a walk, the horses clip-clopping up crescents of clay. It's Felicity who says it.

"Goddamn it, why can't anyone in this fucking family ever *fight!*"

I look over to her. She continues:

"*That's* the problem, you know. Gran and Mother and Pearce can have all the fucking political arguments they want, but they're not talking about anything *important*. Everything's so nonconfrontational. Whenever I try to reason with Mother or tell Pearce to do something with his life, it's like I've violated some secret code that only they know about. Sometimes I feel like some orphan they've kindly taken up off the streets and given shelter. . . . 'Oh, she couldn't possibly know all our rules. Fighting's so *squalid*—we let our lawyers do that.' *I can't stand it!*"

We start to trot. A long pine branch whacks me in the face. Felicity posts, dodging the branch, looking professional even in jeans and a plaid flannel shirt. I'm embarrassed to be wearing breeches since I'm such a slouch on a horse.

"Tighten up on the reins. You won't hurt him." I do as she says. She starts us into a canter. When we're back to a walk, Felicity says, "Mother says I ought never to raise my voice because I sound like a fishwife. She says that if I keep sounding this way I'll end up in a trailer home somewhere with six screaming, dirty children with runny noses, TV on all day, and pots boiling over on the stove. But for God's sake, someone's got to tell her what's best for her, someone besides her doctor. Someone she'll listen to." Felicity pauses. "Look. On the rock to your left," she says, although facing straight ahead. "A rattler."

I turn my head. The snake doesn't move, coiled dull brown in the sun. Barbara told me about the rattlesnake hunts with the groundsmen, the honeycombed tail the prize for whichever child spotted it first.

"So what's with you and Hugh?" I ask.

"What do you mean?"

"Well, you're taking your horses to Florida for the winter, and you'll—"

"Hugh knows where we stand. I see him when I see him. He's free to do whatever he likes." She pauses. "I've been terribly busy."

Tentatively, I ask if Helen's receiving visitors.

"Not yet. The disease embarrasses her, you know. Hates feeling out of control. And she won't believe them when they tell her it's medical, treatable, that something can be *done*. And then when they give her the lithium and she *does* start feeling better, she thinks: 'Ah-hah! I'm better!' And since she won't believe it's medical, she wonders: 'Why this medicine?' Then there goes the lithium, down the toilet."

"I see."

Again there's only the clip-clop of hooves. Then Felicity scrunches up her face as if something has just occurred to her. "Good God," she says. "Mum's even more hardheaded than *me*."

The men are at the stables when we get back. They take the horses to untack.

Walking back to the house, I feel low and stubby in my boots, down from sixteen hands. We reach the lawn, late afternoon sun cutting brilliantly across the grass and

180

three black crows at marsh's edge—pecking, bobbing unsteadily.

"I feel so stunted," I say, "down here on the ground."

"Happens."

Back in the house, pictures and furniture around us, we regain our sense of proportion.

—

There is a story of Felicity in the Bullring. It was in 1978, when Helen was still with her Mr. Bolini; she had her children there with her in Spain. It was at Mr. Bolini's school that Felicity became serious about training professionally. One day she was doing an exhibition, putting horses through their paces against the bulls. Felicity was just thirteen then—a prodigy. When she had finished, the bulls locked away, a friend from the riding school asked, "Who is that woman in the hat who hates you so much?" Without so much as a glance through the crowd, Felicity answered:

"That is my mother."

CUSHIONS

Florida, January 1989

Some line was down, as in a storm.

I don't know where I've read that phrase, but the image stays with me—a cut black cable, trailing down across a highway, disattached.

Gentle gusts of wind blow up from the ocean, muffled flapping from the umbrellaed tables by the pool. Thick, heavy air, but no rain to relieve it. A dirty white sky.

Cousin Felicity pushes back her chair.

"Mum, I'm going back for the salmon mousse. It's good. Wouldn't you like some?"

"No, thank you," says Aunt Helen, stroking the rim of her teacup. Half a Cuban cracker, white crumbs, and an olive pit lie beside it. Her lunch.

Felicity stands to full height and says, "Well, then, I'll have to find something yummy to *surprise* you," and carries her plate toward the buffet.

Sunday brunch at the club—big production. Deviled eggs garnished with pimento crosses lie in untouched symmetry on a platter, beginning to sweat. Beyond these stand bowls of seafood salads, arrangements of cold cuts, piles of icy shrimp and cracked crab claws. Chafing dishes hold browned beef and peeled parsleyed potatoes in oil, warming over blue kerosene flames.

An ice sculpture, shape now indistinguishable, stands at the center of the buffet. A small river flows from its base, guided by a tube running under the tablecloth.

There's a separate dessert table, loaded down with coconut cake and cream pastries slick with melted frosting. There is also a plate of macaroons, a large bowl holding a ladle with floating island in a thick sauce.

Too much food. Too much of everything.

Helen bought her Florida house in 1980 after she and Mr. Bolini separated.

"I don't particularly like the place," she said then, "but it seems to be where old divorced women like me are supposed to go." Helen shipped her furniture and a few pictures, while a friend at Sotheby's wrung his hands about salt corrosion, sent a list of what to keep under glass.

Helen doesn't play tennis or golf, and avoids the sun. When she was well she wore rice powder and pink lipstick. Nothing now.

That morning I'd slept in while Felicity drove to the stables to give a lesson. We'd arranged to meet at the club at twelve.

"Will you be all right looking after her this morning? Maybe take her to church."

The church is a minute from the club, cutting into the fairway. The island roads are designed for golf carts—a fifteen-mile-per-hour speed limit. Sometimes during the week the church parking spills onto the golf course and the club flag flies at half mast, indicating a loss. This is why visiting children call the island "God's waiting room."

We didn't get to church this morning. Aunt Helen did dress herself for lunch, putting on a linen shift and a wide straw hat to shield her face. "Your dress is wrinkled, Ms. Fraser," the nurse said as we left the house. "Let me press it for you."

Helen is smoking a cigarette, something I've never seen her do. Otherwise she looks all right, still so removed from the leathery golfing women who cluster at other tables: small groups of blinding pinks, yellows, greens, drinking gin. Their conversation—low muffled murmurs—doesn't quite waft over. These women have learned to be gentle with each other, have busied themselves with golf and grandchildren, have learned to cushion their blows.

Helen wants a nap ("a nap, in the cool dark"). We leave the club. At the house the dogs and the nurse meet her by the door. The nurse takes her arm.

Felicity lifts her hand from her hip to adjust her dark glasses. She says to me, "I'm going into town to drop off her needlepoint. Want to come?"

Felicity hates Palm Beach.

Shoppers in the muggy lull mill up and down on the short blocks of Worth Avenue, looking at window displays that rarely change. There are too many jewelry stores, not enough cafés. Rows of even palms cut up through the pavement across the white sky—bristling, strategic. Pavement leads to where you can see and smell the sea, but the beach is closed, the doors locked at the breakwater.

At the wall, the views up and down are interrupted by massive metal siphons, sucking up sand at the waterline, funneling back the beach as it slips away. Sucking up and spitting out, like giant black elephant trunks. Back up the avenue, the shops sell pink-and-white ceramic end tables shaped like elephants, these alongside white patent purses and painted French cachepots. "Worthless Avenue."

Going into the needlepoint shop, Felicity mentions, "The doctor says it's all right to have needles, so long as she stays stable."

A kind-looking woman with slow hands and white hair in a flip greets Felicity and asks her about the stables. Felicity takes from her bag a finished canvas—cross-shaped, about a foot wide, an underwater scene of the ocean floor. Small happy pink fishes and a beige seahorse float on an aqua-blue ground. The shop lady wraps the corners of the canvas around a brick, showing us how nice it will look as a doorstop. Felicity chooses a blue felt backing, and the woman says she'll phone when it's ready.

We poke around the shop, Felicity flipping through a pile of painted canvases.

"I try to avoid the ones with much background, because she won't finish those." Aunt Helen had never done needlepoint until Silver Hill, where Felicity brought her kits, explaining, "She didn't hate it as much as I thought she might."

Felicity chooses a cushion-sized canvas of a German shepherd, says that with darker colors it could look like

Guinness. The shop lady looks for yarn and says it might be a while. I'm feeling faint, so Felicity and I walk two doors down to a chrome and glass restaurant where everything on the menu is served stuffed into a croissant. We order iced teas with large wedges of lemon. Felicity tells me a lot of things, matter-of-factly, as we sit by the window.

"Before Mum was hospitalized, the painful thing was that, rationally, she could see that she was not rational. Rationally, she knows she's got to take the medicine to stay well, but some perverse bravery makes her want to go without."

I nod.

"You see," Felicity continues, "she's terrified that she'll kill herself. When I first signed her into the hospital, she wouldn't talk. She just grunted like an animal, distraught and clawing. She called out all night that she wanted to die. Then she thought the nurses were trying to poison her."

From Linc, I knew that Helen was afraid. At first Helen thought that anything the nurses served her was horse meat, that they were feeding her her own horses. The only person she'd let feed her was her daughter, spoonful by spoonful, because she knew that Felicity wouldn't stand to see a horse slaughtered. Afterward Felicity would exit, gamely telling the doctor, "Still hates me, but she's fed."

"For someone afraid of being poisoned," I say to Felicity, "it sounds like she wanted very badly to live."

Felicity pokes at her ice with the straw, jabbing the lemon slice. "Well, now she's just living *badly*. I don't know if it's an improvement. But she wants to be near Pearce, and Pearce wants to be based here. Not that he's around much. He's afraid that he might see her sick again."

"She seems O.K. here. . . ."

"It's no good for her. This padded environment is just not her. *Needlepoint* is just not her. She feels caged, watched, when taking the medicine. She *appears* back to her old self, but down inside she thinks the pills make her helpless . . . much more so than before, when she was too paranoid to ride in a car or stand in a group. You see, back then the threats were from outside the body. Now we've invited the doctors *in*. But what else could I do?"

I think of last night, looking through the albums—photos from early in the marriages, photos of Helen and the children. There were patches of glue where some pictures had been torn out, or half of a photo sliced off. Felicity walked in on me.

"Mum used to get at these with scissors," she'd said. "It's the ones of her that are missing."

We finish our iced tea and stop to pick up the new canvas and yarn, buy Helen's shampoo at Saks. Felicity drops me at the house around four, drives back to the stables. Helen's not up from her nap. The nurse is watching a Western.

No one else on the beach. The sky has gone purple—grey, small gusts of wind, otherwise quiet.

Seagulls leave shallow claw marks on the hard wet sand, their folded wings grey like the sky. They don't seem to know where to go.

I hold my shoes behind my back, walking in the water—the shallowest point, where the sliver of tide rushes gently before it recedes. A narrow line of tiny white and brown shell fragments rolls slightly with each wave.

The houses are quiet, shut up far behind the concrete seawall and close-cropped lawns. The grass here, although short, is spiky and hard—dark-green spears, points blunted by mowers. The roots lie above the earth, like sod.

Rolls and rolls of sod laid down on the salt-seeped soil. That's why the lawns bounce when you walk on them— cushiony sod, dead and dry.

I pass the beach club, quiet, not even kids in the pool. Farther up the shore, two ladies walk slowly in sweatpants and running shoes.

The sea ripples slightly around my feet. A gull caws, breaking the silence.

Suddenly, a shooting pain. The water rushes back as I look down to see what has happened. A blue bubble clings at my left ankle, wrapped tight. I shake the foot, run back into the water. The next wave catches the man-o'-war and carries it away. I stand there, clutching my ankle, rubbing the wet skin. The tentacles have left two lines of pin-sized blue dots around my ankle. I rub again and dunk the foot, trying to wash off the sting.

It's not bad, I think, and turn, heading back to the house. Nearing the club I feel dizzy and have to sit on the sand. When I get up, nausea hits. By the time I reach the pool, the empty lifeguard stand, my thigh's cramped up, muscles tighten around the groin.

"A man-o'-war . . ." I say to the woman who hands out the towels.

"Just a little one," she says, bending over my foot. "But best get you to the nurse." She gives me a towel and I realize I'm sweating cold buckets.

The rows of dots have risen to form welts, small pillows of pain.

The nurse makes a paste of meat tenderizer and water, packs it onto my foot with gauze bandages.

"Not the season for them," the towel lady says to the nurse.

"Caught you good, didn't it?" says the nurse.

And they have me lie down while in the next room

they tell stories of people with large ropes of tentacle wrapped around their abdomen, people in worse shape than I.

—

Nights now I've had crying jags—unexpected, heavy, brief, like a sudden rain. I don't know what is wrong, but I know that it's groundless and to wait it out. I hold my head under a pillow so that no one will hear the childish, chest-heaving sobs. Soon the tears subside. I take off the pillow and gasp for breath.

—

The next morning, early, I take my tea onto the porch. Felicity's gone to the stables, the house is quiet, the breeze gentle.

Tenderly, I touch my ankle, stroking the swollen ridge.

Things catch you.

For weeks after, the skin is scarred numb. Then slowly, predictably, the feeling starts coming back.

—

I never thought of my mother as having gone crazy. Just that things didn't work out for her.

It looked for a while as if she was going to get better. She had her vegetable garden in Papa's Palo Alto backyard, safe in shady suburbs spawned by the university. She would be down on the ground as she'd been at the farm, tugging on weeds between haphazard rows of vegetables, still trying to produce something.

But most of the time she was in bed—shades down, an electric heater on the bare floor (the small, glowing kind with a low hum and zigzag of red wire).

"Your mother's run down," my father would say be-

fore canceling an out-of-town lecture, because without him Mama couldn't sleep at all.

"Doctors don't know what it is," my mother would say, although she hadn't seen one in years. There was a woman, though, who sent vitamins, astrological charts and cassettes once a month. My father would brew ginseng tea for my mother while she would do her yoga, chanting on the bedroom floor. It scared me at that age to hear her chant, like noise rising from the crypt in a horror movie.

In the mornings before going to work, my father would steam vegetables and brown rice for her because she said preservatives made her crazy and sugar made her tired. But one afternoon he came home and found the kitchen hot and full of smells and her at the table with a plate of hash brownies, reading my copy of Misty of Chincoteague.

My father didn't fight with her, but in a way he gave up—"There was just no more I could do." One morning soon after my tenth birthday we woke to find she'd disappeared. A week later he got a note from a holistic retreat in Oregon. "I need a rest and don't come get me," was the gist. She had done things like this before and then come back, standing with her leather knapsack on the doorstep. But this time it got to be a month, then two months, and when my father did try to find her she'd left for the West Indies.

The pumpkins and squash did well that fall. But neither my father nor I much knew what to do with them, save letting them rot on the vine.

I used to tell myself I wasn't angry. That, like my father, I'd given her up long before. From an early age I'd learned to love her memory, not her presence. "There is nothing brutal about the expected."

We did not see her at the end, and I did not cry when Papa told me she had died. Of malnutrition, of all things.

LUXE,
CALME,
VOLUPTÉ

New York, May 1989

The doorman reminds me about the storage space. The board has sent out notices; all residents must remove their belongings from basement storage, the area is to be converted for a new boiler.

The building porter shows me down. The space is bare except for a few old suitcases, two cardboard boxes marked "Kitchen," and a stack of dirty window screens. The porter helps load these into the service elevator.

I move the things into the spare room, dusting with a paper towel.

Two of the suitcases are Gran's—dark, hard-sided leather, heavy and empty.

There is also a smaller suitcase—cheap red plaid vinyl.

I put the suitcase on the bed and unzip it. Gingerly, I sift through the items, most of them familiar.

Contents: one stained Indian blouse, a tattered gauze skirt, stick incense, scratchy wool socks, a jar of vitamin C—rosehip tablets, birth control pills, a good boar-bristle hairbrush, two pamphlets from a meditational center near Tallahassee, and a pair of brown leather snowboots, long out of fashion.

The expiration date on the birth control packet reads "3/78." She left this suitcase for storage. I take a deep breath, and then an hour has passed.

A week later. I check the clock. The Roman numerals are still glowing green from the last time I turned on the light.

It's been four nights now like this. Even when I'm able to drift off, I wake minutes later, my heart pumping fast as I lie dead still, trying to remember sleep.

It's about the oral presentation. Or at least it started that way. The French Symbolist seminar, a forty-five-minute talk on Mallarmé. I've never talked for forty-five minutes.

The first night I lay awake, I kept pad and paper by my bedside. My head was full of ideas, new avenues for the talk. I'd get up and jot them down.

By the third night I was too exhausted to sleep; my research reached dead ends. I turned clumsy—five bruises now on my shins, thigh, and arm, turning from a deep purply-red to a deep purply-green. The one on my arm is from the bath faucet, a bizarre fall. I've been taking a lot of hot baths, but those seem to help only until I'm dry.

In a fog, I raised my hand to push my hair from my face and, with a broken nail, scratched a red gash across my cheek just under the eye. The scratch didn't bleed, but tiny points of blood dotted the line, pooling just beneath the last layer of skin.

I walk home through the park with John from writing class. John, I would say, is my closest friend from Columbia. It is a perfect spring day.

"See a shrink," says John, wiping his glasses with a handkerchief. "Isn't that what you people do?"

"I don't need a shrink." I turn to look behind us. There is only a woman in a rose sweatsuit, walking a dachshund. She takes folded sheets of paper toweling from her pocket.

"He'd give you something for your nerves."

"Huh?"

"A psychiatrist would give you something to help your nerves."

"Drugs? I don't do drugs."

"Just some sleeping pills or something."

"I will be fine once this presentation is done with."

"Then maybe if you start seeing him or her on a regular basis, they could help you learn to let go of whatever it is that's—"

"The thing about this presentation is that it's completely *written*, except for that bit tying the journey poems with . . . but that's central to . . . God, you don't want to hear this. It's a synthesis problem, and I'm usually good at synthesis—"

"You know, girl, you're losing your mind. . . ."

"I just can't stand in front of a whole room of people the way I am now; I absolutely can't."

"Have you thought to—"

As I turn to look back, John catches my arm and spins me around. "Meredith, will you please *stop* that while I'm talking to you?"

"I thought someone was following us."

"You are becoming a *serious* threat."

That evening I call Connecticut. Gran never will use the phone on account of her deafness. But Sylvie says it would be fine and that George will meet my train.

Next day, stepping off onto the platform at Westport, I feel immediately better. The trees seem big and old, the leaves showing their silvery undersides in the wind. How silly I've been.

George takes my knapsack of books and my overnight bag, puts them in the trunk. I ride in the back seat, watching the mailboxes on Garrett Road speed by.

We pass through the main gates, up the drive that cuts through a field.

The glass panes of the fanlight over the front door sparkle. Sylvie's in the doorway, with her white uniform and running shoes. George leaves my bags in the front hall, while Sylvie clasps her hands and explains that my grandmother is tired, that Gran and I will each be taking our dinner on trays and will see each other tomorrow.

Upstairs, Sylvie shows me into a pretty rose-patterned bedroom.

"This is room your aunt Helen stay in—she say was only room with hard enough mattress."

"I think I'll be very comfortable. Thank you, Sylvie."

"Mrs. Fraser, she hasn't been here for a while, but . . . last time she stay? She didn't sleep in no bed, she slept, you know, on the bathmat. I find her like that when I bring in her tray in the morning, she say, 'Sylvie, the beds here are too soft.' "

"Aunt Helen slept in the bathroom?"

"Yes, I find her all curled up like that, on the mat."

When Sylvie leaves I walk into the bathroom, turn on the light. I have a thought, and I quietly check the other bedrooms on the second floor, the other bathrooms. I let out a breath when I see it's true: Aunt Helen could feel safe only in the room with no window.

After dinner the house is quiet. There is no TV except for the Zenith in the kitchen. I have my books, I keep to myself.

I hear Gran's night nurse come in, but don't see her. It becomes terribly quiet.

At ten o'clock I take a bath, put on my nightgown, get into bed.

By one o'clock I'm walking the house. The back stairs smell of laundry. The alarm lights glow small and red.

I eat some cereal, wash the bowl, and climb the stairs.

I wake again at four, doze until five. From five on, I lie still. At seven-thirty I hear voices. When I do rise, I am gentle with myself. My body throbs, feeling spent.

After a warm bath, I put on a white shirt, soft clean khakis and pad downstairs.

I hear George's gentle Irish in the kitchen. He comes in at eight every morning and reads the *Daily News* aloud to Sylvie while she soaps the dishes.

Sylvie tells me to sit in the living room, where she'll bring me my tray. One poached egg, toast, bacon, milk, tea, and a small glass of orange juice, with etched leaves circling the rim. The tray linens are a sunny Porthault print, soft from washing. I sit on the sofa, my back to the bay window. Warm morning light hits my shoulders, my neck, making everything seem all right as I break the egg's quivering yolk.

When I'm finished I carry my tray into the kitchen, and Sylvie says no, no, that she's to do that. Then I climb the stairs back to the rose bedroom. My footsteps are muffled by carpet; the house is quiet again.

I feel better, with the sunlight. The pillow feels soft and cottony on my cheek as I lie, stretched facedown, on the white Marseilles coverlet.

The air conditioner—the old-fashioned kind—hums steadily and every now and then gives a kick.

———

There is that awful fairy tale "The Princess and the Pea." I try to remember the point of it. Princesses are sensitive, yes, but is it from their thin blood or does it come from years of pampering, no bumps? As soon as a pea-sized problem comes along, they're bruised and exhausted. . . .

I picture Helen in 1963. Helen who didn't go to college, didn't have to give classroom presentations. Helen married and went to London, danced the twist at Diamonds, the nightclub with the spiral staircase. Her evening clothes would have been set out on her bed by a ladies' maid; at seven o'clock Helen would sit in her slip at a vanity table as the maid combed out her hair.

———

It is so quiet here. There is that tendency to repeat music in your head, the last song you've heard.

What I heard in the cab driving down to Grand Central. Something about sympathy . . . luxury . . . somebody to care for me. I know I have the words wrong, but the lines play over until finally I drift off.

There are things I've been noticing lately, images stored, appearing in half-sleep:

196

The sun is high, the pool sparkles pale blue beyond the cabanas. Two women are propped up in chaise longues, reading magazines, sucking pink drinks through straws. They are maybe twenty-six, with just the beginning of crepeyness under their eyes, behind the dark glasses. One wears a tiny Lilly Pulitzer bikini, her tan stomach bulging slightly. The other one wears a checked cotton skirted suit, the kind with boning, the kind that mothers wear.

The one in the skirted suit gives a curled-fingered wave to a white-capped toddler and his au pair, who's blowing up water wings at the edge of the wading pool.

The bikinied woman spreads tanning oil on her legs and stomach. A dragonfly with large, clear wings lights on the edge of her chaise; she shoos it away. She places the bottle on the small glass-topped table and wipes the oil from her hands.

Her friend has picked up Town & Country.

The girls have an acquaintance on the cover, a red-haired girl who looks like Lulu. According to the credits, the cover girl is wearing an emerald dog collar from Harry Winston and Chanel Super Hydrabase lipstick in Soleil Mirage.

"It says here she's twenty-two," says the skirted-suit girl.

"Twenty-two in model years. That's twenty-six to you and me," says the tan girl.

On the cover, block blue letters read: "Town & Country's Exclusive Guide to Psychotherapy."

The child screams from the wading pool.

The skirt-suited girl flips through the remaining pages, then picks Time off the hot concrete. The water-stained pages are folded back to the "Law" section, an article on postpartum women who drown their babies.

Felicity comes in for lunch, looking tall and thin in breeches and boots. Gran joins us at the dining room table. Sylvie is glad, says we're having a real Saturday lunch party.

Afterward Gran retires and Felicity and I sit in the book-lined study. Felicity asks:

"What did you do to your face?" (Not "What happened?" but "What did you *do?*")

I put my hand to my cheek.

"Scratched myself. I've been sort of a mess."

We discuss the French Symbolists. Felicity seems to know more than I. I change the subject.

"How's Hugh?"

"It's finished," she says.

"Oh. I'm sorry. . . ."

"That's all right. It was a bad situation."

"I liked him."

"It had reached a crisis point."

"Because you wouldn't move to Seattle?"

"It was a bit more complicated." Felicity takes a deep breath, then says, "You know how I didn't want to have children?"

"He objected to that?"

"Ideally, he wouldn't have. But what we had last month was *not* an ideal situation."

"Oh . . . I'm sorry," I say, realizing, guessing. "I'm so sorry. . . ."

"It's O.K. now. Situation resolved."

"How do you feel?"

Felicity shrugs. "Didn't miss a day of work."

"Well. That's good."

After some silence, Felicity says, "I've got to get back to the stables. Let's keep in touch this time."

"Yes, let's."

The next morning I take the train back to the city. Monday I give the presentation. Monday night I sleep fine.

"See? It was all situational," I tell John Tuesday.

He looks at me queerly.

———

Weeks later I read a magazine article on insomnia. The author suggests picturing a calm, peaceful place.

When I try this the images that come surprise me—they are of Oregon, of my mother's farm. Low gray skies and orchard road, forgotten plains of high grass, fallen fences. The wet carpet of leaves deep within the black forest, the pale moss clinging to the north side of trees down by the creek where we'd caught salamanders in a jar and set them free.

SUMMER
GAMES III

Maine, August 1989

Water still clings to the snapdragons as I cut, scattering drops onto my tennis shoes. I'm tentative with the scissors, taking flowers from where they grow thick, careful not to leave a spot bare. I've got Helen's long wicker flower basket hooked over my arm, and I think of how Helen used to cut, quick snips along the branch.

I still hesitate before each cut. I wonder if this caution would change if the garden were mine.

Helen is better—"A-OK!" said a friend of Gran's. Helen was here last week with a new, shorter haircut, worry lines vanished. This week she's in Bridgehampton, visiting a friend over from England.

Felicity's training an Olympic alternate; hasn't been up this summer. It's just Pearce and me this particular weekend.

The yacht club porch, usual table. Light fog and blackberry pie. The Lowes ask about my plans after college.

"I'm interested in journalism, mostly . . . maybe grad school, after a year I don't know."

"We call this the what-to-do-when-you-don't-have-to-do-anything thing," says Billy, tapping his coffee spoon.

"When you can do anything, you have to be especially sure to choose something," says Amanda.

Billy turns to her admiringly. "Very good."

"Remember, you have no excuse not to make your life special," Amanda says, absently sliding her gold bracelet up and down her wrist, a series of half turns.

Pearce returns with a cup of coffee.

"What's special?"

"Meredith's choices. For next year."

"Which choices?"

"Internships," I say. "Maybe GMATs."

"You know, Pearce," says Billy. "The work ethic thing."

"No, I wouldn't know about that."

"Come on, be serious," says Amanda. "Meredith's impressionable."

Billy turns to me, tries to look solemn. "Meredith. Do you know the absolute number-one driving motivational force behind success?"

"What's that?"

" 'Cause it'll piss off your parents."

The three laugh uneasily.

• • •

Later that afternoon Pearce says, "Let's go to the mainland for dinner."

Pearce has bought a cigarette boat. He looks funny untying it—a drug runner moored between the Atchesons' wooden catboat and children's turnabouts.

He wants to try a restaurant that's opened next to the one that once wouldn't sell him mussels.

He drives to the float to pick me up, cuts the engine. He holds out both hands so that I can pass him his pitcher of planter's and stack of plastic tumblers. He secures these below as I hop on.

The air is wet, but there is no rain. We wear yellow slickers anyway, with the way Pearce drives—accelerating over waves, slapping water hard as we come down, cold spray over the sides.

I agree that the place is stupid-looking—dark wood and stained glass. As soon as we're seated Pearce excuses himself. "Back in a minute. Order a drink."

He leaves the restaurant. I order a grapefruit juice.

Returning twenty minutes later, he says he's changed his mind. Scooting into his chair, he says we're going back home to eat with the Lowes, but late. So for now we'll order something to tide us over, "just to get something in your stomach."

The waiter approaches, and Pearce asks me what I want.

"The cheddar potato skins, please."

"Good," says Pearce. "Mixing proteins and carbs."

After the waiter leaves I ask, "Pearce. What's going on?"

Evil smile. "Just you wait."

. . .

The boat's got radar so that he can find the island coming back after dark. Tonight it's foggy as well, and Pearce screams instructions as he hands me the wheel. He ducks below deck to check one of the machines. The air in front of us is thick white, the boat lights bounce off the fog. I'm terrified at the controls. Finally, he takes the wheel, tells me to hang on tight because he'd lose me if I fell overboard. When Pearce thinks he's found the north point of the island he speeds up, crashing through swells, heavy spray. I crawl along the floor, gripping a cleat, trying to lie flat.

We pass through another boat's wake. Pearce slows a bit before saying, "Funny. No boat showing on radar . . ." He hums the theme from *The Twilight Zone*.

"Are you sure? Is it working?"

"Not sure. Can't see it. Hah! Hold on!" He guns it; we reach such a speed that I can barely hear him when he yells, "Now where is that damn island? Know I left it here somewhere. . . ."

We're sure to die. The pitcher of planter's has splashed over the deck; the rail is sticky under my grip until the salt spray washes it clean. The vinyl-coated pillows, though slippery wet, are strapped tight. I cling for dear life.

Suddenly, he slows, we bob for a minute, he cuts the engine. Dead quiet, except for water lapping on the sides. The front spotlights barely cut within throwing distance—twin shafts of bright fog, circles on the water. Pearce's voice carries back.

"Still all right?" he asks.

"Fine," I answer, shaken, wet.

"Good. Some people find they have to throw up about half an hour into it."

"I don't get seasick."

"I'm not talking about the boat." Pearce stares straight at me. "Tell me, dear Meredith, how, exactly, do you feel right now?"

Still lying flat on the wet cushions, I stare back. "What do you mean?"

Pearce smiles and shrugs.

"You're kidding." I say this without emotion.

He shrugs again, looking pleased with himself.

"You know I don't do that stuff."

"What stuff?" Mock innocence.

It is possible he is just teasing.

"You know what I mean," I say. "You know I don't do drugs."

"Not yet . . ."

"Did you put something in the food?"

"You should never leave for the ladies' room while a meal is arriving. It's rude."

"I do hope you're joking."

"Not saying a word."

"Are you doing it now? Is that why we had to go to the mainland? To pick it up?"

He shrugs and moves to the highest point of the bow, stretches his arms up, links his hands on top of his head, turns a half circle and says:

"You know, I don't have a fucking clue where we are. . . ."

I put my face between my hands, breathe deeply. I am shivering from the cold but now feel hot points of panic flashing through.

Anger can wait. I look up, take another breath. "Just get me to shore. Then tell me what to expect."

Pearce starts the engine, changes direction. In minutes, we reach the north point.

We tie the boat at the base of our own dockless pier. The house is hidden by the fog. After tying up, Pearce removes his shoes and jumps into the freezing water, surfaces, and yelps, shaking his head.

"Water's great!" he calls.

I slip off the side of the boat. When my toes touch bottom I do not feel them. The cold numbs my body as I swim swiftly to shore.

Pearce says it's as if a soft velvet cloak has fallen gently over his head. We're curled up on the sofa in our soft dry clothes. Billy Lowe is on Pearce's other side, smile fixed tight across his face, while Amanda lies like a cat across Billy's lap, making purry little sighing sounds. Cassette tapes lie scattered on the floor, and the logs burn low while the four of us snuggle deeper into the sofa, me with both arms hugging a pillow and Pearce's head resting, rocking slightly, on my shoulder.

"Darling pussycat," Billy whispers to his wife. He's sipping brandy from a large snifter, and I think how lovely the gold color looks glowing firelight.

She whispers something to him, and he nods.

When I see them out the door, Amanda asks me, "Are you all right?"

"I hope so," I answer. "Are you O.K. to drive?"

"Oh, well, actually . . . yes." Amanda glances at Billy, who's pulled their jeep up. "We're not doing it. The pills he gave Bill are wrapped in a napkin by the bar."

"You didn't take them?"

"No. We just don't. But this time we played along."

"Right."

"You sure you'll be O.K.?" Amanda looks concerned.

It is too late to tell her what happened, that this was

not a choice I'd made. I say, "Yeah . . . fine," and leave it at that.

I go into the living room to say good night, but Pearce says, "Stay another minute, because I've got to tell you something."

"Then tell me quick, because I'm going to bed."

He sits me down.

"I'm telling you you're *not* going to bed."

I stand up. "Yes I am."

"No. It's really important that I talk to you."

"You have one minute."

He stays silent for a moment, that same fixed smile. Then he pulls a snapdragon from the bowl on the coffee table. Squeezing the yellow bud with his fingers, he makes the dragon's mouth and pinches my arm with it, whispering:

"It's biting you! It's biting you!"

———

An unsettled dream:

"So what is it you want?" I ask.

He looks straight at me.

I say, "That won't solve anything."

He takes a move closer. "No?" The smooth tan of his face cracks, while the part near his left eye twitches, convulses.

Flowers grow on the abyss slope. We are traveling over a pit. The petals begin to move, then eyes and nostrils appear. Tiny forked points begin to wave, and the flowers become rows of dragon faces, mouths open and beckoning.

I am frozen, no breath to cry for help. I don't even try—the air is thin and weak and would not carry the call. It seems as if we're spinning down in a circle; part of me

wakes and knows these are bedspins, that I'm asleep, that
I'm alone, that this is not a closed circle, but then—
faintly—I hear again:
"You know, I don't have a fucking clue where we
are!"

———

I am wide awake as the door creaks. My head is suddenly clear.

"Get out," I say, not moving, heart pounding.

He sits on the edge of the bed, ignoring me, rubbing his head. He is disheveled, wet-looking, his hair matted. There is a new smell in the room, something rank.

"It's four in the morning," I say, sitting up, moving away.

"Is that what you sleep in?" he asks, looking down at my thin white T-shirt, the outline of my breasts.

I gather the covers around me. "Sometimes."

He nods appraisingly.

The rank smell I noticed lingers—like shored fish or seaweed, something dead.

I notice the twitch.

"Go to bed," I say.

He closes his eyes and lies down on top of my covers. I sit upright, back against the headboard and look down at him.

"I didn't mean here."

Asleep, still twitching, he lies heavy as a corpse, and I cannot move him.

So this is what 7:00 A.M. looks like. Warmer this morning, the fog hanging close.

The rough, grainy surface of the diving board grips tight to my skin, seeming to hold me. Felicity's white terry

robe and a dry towel cover me as I lie facedown, flat atop
the board.

From the diving board I can see across the lawn to
the sea drop. Along the ledge, the gardener and his machine have missed some cutting. A fringe of taller grass
remains; the white tops of Queen Anne's lace grow wild
out of the rocky steep.

The water meets the dove white fog. Further out, a
lobster buoy bobs suspended in the mist. Except for the
nearest slow morning ripples, the sea can't be seen, only
heard; a high, gentle pitch like chimes wrapped in gauze.

But then again I hear the grinding of my teeth, my
head pounding. I click my jaw back and forth, roll my
shoulders, unknotting the muscles.

So this was how Harry felt? I'd kill myself too.

But I remember that this was not my fault. Not
entirely.

The pain is sharp in my head, and under my breath I
begin to whisper the following:

"I'm going to kill him. I'm going to kill him. . . ."

Hours later, not napping but eyes closed.

Pearce's voice. *"There* you are." I look up. Pearce is
wearing a white terry robe like mine, a towel over his
shoulders.

I do not respond.

"So—good morning, and how are *you*," he asks.

"All right," I say tightly.

"Red wine, a nice lunch, then a nap, and you'll be all
fixed up."

I say nothing.

Pearce puts his towel to his face, gets a funny look,
and sniffs the towel. "Goddamnit," he cries. "Stella's been

using those dryer sheets again. I've *told* her not to. This towel smells like the inside of a Haitian cab.''

''Do you always have to talk like that?'' I snap.

''What's with you? Sheesh.'' Pearce rubs his face and yawns, sitting down on the edge of the teak deck chair, pushing back the sodden white-duck cushion.

Where to start, I think, but the time has passed.

After a minute, another yawn and stretch, he asks, ''Who do you want for lunch?''

''I don't care. I'm leaving.''

''I think we'll do ribs.'' Pearce then sits silently on the edge of the deck chair.

I catch a whiff of his cologne from last night, faint and rank. I bury my face between my arms to escape. The smell is stronger. I'm confused for a moment, sniff again. I realize then that the smell is on my own skin. A wave of nausea passes, and I grip the board.

He gets up, then asks, ''Are you going for a swim?''

''Yes. I think so.''

''Sounds good.'' He turns and starts back up toward the house. Three steps. Then he turns and, walking backward, calls out, ''That was fun last night, wasn't it?''

I nod but turn my head away, facing the ocean. The time for anger has passed, and I missed it.

Delta has a two o'clock out of Bangor. With the fog, I can take the ferry, then a cab. Yes, before lunch, I think, definitely before lunch.

LOSING

TOUCH

New York, October 1989

Tom McPhearson's firm is in midtown,
my appointment is at two.

His secretary seems to know me. Mr. McPhearson
comes out and shows me back to his office. His desk is
clear except for pens, a notepad. Behind it is a dizzying
drop of floor-to-ceiling glass.

"How's school?"

"Fine."

"You're graduating this spring?"

"Yes."

"What did you study?"

"Journalism."

"Super. Uh-huh." Mr. McPhearson plays with a sleek

ballpoint pen, suspending it lengthwise between two fingers. "And your father," he asks, "how's he doing?"

"He's fine."

"Still out in California?"

I nod.

"I hear you've got your own place now."

I nod. "It's closer to school."

He smiles. Then—as if by afterthought—produces the papers. I sign quickly.

"So where do you want it sent?" he asks.

"I don't know. Where do you think?"

"Depends on your objectives."

"I really don't know yet. . . ."

"When you decide, let me know, and we'll have it wired."

"All right."

"Do you have a CPA?"

"No."

Mr. McPhearson gives me the name of Felicity's. We chat a minute more. He is very nice. I say thank you as I leave; he says, "Happy birthday."

Out the elevator and through the glass-walled atrium, the jungle of trees, I find myself on Park Avenue. It's just beginning to rain, large splatters against my suit. Fallen leaves blow on the pavement in fast circles. I feel I should do something to celebrate, but I've made no plans. I look for a cab with its light on, but the cabs are full. I take a crosstown bus home.

I'd known for a while it was time to leave. My rental studio off West End Avenue has a view across the Hudson: tall Jersey smokestacks, factory smoke. Except for a mattress and box spring, I've bought no furniture.

I sit on the bed with my mail. The post office forwards

it; a system of yellow labels, the new address in gray dot matrix.

Electric bill, bank statement. A white envelope from Helen, who is in Maine, closing up the house. I recognize the card from The Island Store: mice dressed in T-shirts and fishing caps, rowing a canoe. "Happy Wishes—Aunt Helen" is all she has written inside.

My father telephones, as does John. Pearce does not.

Two days later, the middle of the night.

I wake suddenly, agitated, feeling I have to move around. I try to lie still in bed, but feel ill, panicked. I get up to heat some milk. After drinking it, I make myself lie down again, trying to relax, breathe evenly. But something in me is keenly alert, aware of each breath. It is unlike any feeling I have had before. I am suddenly, wholly, aware that there is something that has happened and that I do not yet know what it is.

The clock says two. I reach for the telephone on the floor and dial my father. He's on West Coast time, the only person I know I won't wake.

"Papa?"

"Meredith?"

"Yes."

"What's wrong?"

"I don't know. *God, I just don't know.*"

The phone rings at eight the next morning.

"Hello?"

There's static on the line. "Oh," a girl's voice says, "did I wake you? What is it—like nine there?"

"Um. It's . . ."

"Sorry. I thought you people who had school would be up. Listen, it's *Lulu*. Pearce is being *weird*. I mean, you're saying, Hey, what's new, but last night he didn't come back—"

"Lulu, where are you?"

"Madrid. And I can tell you this is the most god-awful place. No one speaks English. I spend all this time trying to get the operator or room service to do *anything*, and it's me talking real slowly and loudly in English, thinking that's going to help. Turns out Pearce has us checked in as Mr. and Mrs. Bennett, which is totally bizarre, because that's like the sort of thing that would make him *freak* if I suggested it. So I told them my name and *none* of them had a *clue* but then the concierge spoke perfect English and is just, like, this lovely man, and now my new best friend."

"So how's Madrid?" I say, waking up.

"You have to understand, Pearce *kidnapped* me after lunch the other day. I mean, it's Have lunch with Pearce, wake up in Spain. We were at Bilbouquet, right? With that gossip columnist friend of his. Do you read his column? Well, I said I wanted an iced tea and excused myself to the ladies' room and when I get back there's this ugly orange drink at my place—'Special French aperitif,' Pearce says. So I drink this nasty Frog drink, which is something *fierce*, and then Pearce gets this look in his eye and says, "Lulu, are you feeling adventurous?" I nod, and he says, 'With passport ready?' I whip it out 'cause this is kind of a joke between us. Anyway that columnist, Robert, was watching all this, so check the paper, probably today's—"

"So after lunch . . ."

"O.K., so Pearce gets me into this limo and we cross some bridge and I realize what's going on—why else would Pearce go to, like, *Queens?* I *beg* him to let me go home and pack, but he says he'll buy me clothes when we get where we're going. So I say, Well, in that case I certainly hope we're going to *Paris*. So we arrive at Kennedy, and I think we're going to Paris, but then we get to the counter and they say that flight is all booked in first class and Pearce won't fly business or coach and there's this other flight to *Spain* and I say yuck, but Pearce is psyched, says it's really cool in Spain—I mean, he had *his* bags, he was all set. So here we are . . . or here I am, at least."

"Lulu, what—"

"I mean, I still feel like hell, and I'm trapped here at the Ritz, staring at the ceiling watching goddamned Euro MTV. I have no cash, and I've been washing my face with Pearce's soap, which I *swear* I'm allergic to . . . these little red bumps—"

I interrupt. "What's happened to Pearce?"

"Oh, he's completely crazed. We get here and I wanted to nap and he *throws* his briefcase across the room 'cause he thinks he's lost his Mont Blanc—I mean, the boy loses a pen and he's crazed all afternoon; you know how he does stuff when he's really tired—so for dinner we go to some three-star and I'm feeling ill, so I say, 'Just a salad,' and he got furious. Then after dinner he wanted to go to this club and I said I thought we should go to bed like good little girls and boys and he said fine and then when he drops me off at the hotel, he keeps the cab and keeps on going, like he's teaching me a lesson. So I go to bed, but when I wake up one of his bags was missing, no note or anything. . . . I mean, I don't even have my plane ticket, I don't know if he's still in the country or lying in some gutter somewhere. . . ."

I get Lulu's number and tell her everything will be all right. "Go out, get some air, go to the Prado."

"The what?"

. . .

I'm a mess in Blake seminar, half asleep. My afternoon class is canceled. I head home, collapse on my bed, push Playback for messages.

Only one, from Linc—careful and serious. He says: "It's noon. I'm leaving the office now. Call me at home."

"She wouldn't have felt pain," says Linc. "She just drifted off to sleep."

"But I thought she was better. . . . She had gotten better."

"Well, it's not catching any of us by surprise, but . . . anyway." Linc's voice becomes efficient. "Listen, Meredith, we've been looking for Pearce. Any idea?"

"Yes." And I tell my uncle what Lulu told me. I give him her number at the Ritz.

"Not that she's the right person with the news, but who would be?"

"God-awful job," he says.

"What did you say to Gran?"

"Felicity's with her. She wanted to tell her the truth, but then we decided to say 'heart failure' and leave it at that."

Heart failure. "Yes, I see."

Down, as in a storm.

STUMBLING

New York, three days later

A driver, not George, comes around to my apartment. We drive out to Kennedy to pick up Pearce.

The driver hoists Pearce's bags into the trunk. They're exactly like mine. Heavy T. Anthony bags, a late birthday present from Aunt Helen two years ago. Helen had seen my old luggage at Heyton Hall, and said that, like it or not, one's bags will introduce one wherever one goes, so now didn't it make sense to have nice ones? Good God.

Pearce talks as we drive into the city. Talks slowly and raggedly. A tight mumble. He's arranged a dinner.

His eyes look red and sunken. His suit and face droop. We speak only of arrangements, only of the next few hours.

This is where everything wells up, on those lines and then the great organ's last great booming chorus. Felicity chose the music, and I know she must have considered these lines, must have meant to say these things. And I see that she is as sad and as angry as I.

As we walk out, Felicity gives me a strong hug. Pearce, missing a step, stumbles. And we all three blink in the sunshine.

June 1990
Taking Care

GRAN

Westport, Connecticut

"Now, you won't drive too fast, will you, Mrs. Fraser?"

Elizabeth Stewart Fraser, poised at the steering wheel, turns to her nurse and says, "Yes, I most likely will."

The nurse clings to the sides of her seat as the green golf cart takes a tree root with a bounce, rounds a corner with speed.

They go at eight, before the heat. Gran drives at top speed, air hitting her in the face as the cart rolls round the pond. Sometimes a grandchild or Sylvie will perch in back, where the clubs would go, but this morning it is just Gran and the nurse.

"Now, Mrs. Fraser," says the nurse, in a nursery voice,

"let's look for Tommy the atomic turtle. You remember when we saw the turtle in the pond last week. Let's see if we can spot him today. . . ."

The pond is still. Blithe ducks paddle atop stagnant water, algae heavy, blanketing half.

The ride lasts just a few minutes.

"You tired, Mrs. Fraser?"

"Yes, I am."

"Time for our rest?"

"Time for our rest."

George sits in the kitchen with coffee and the *Daily News*. Once a week he puts on a dark suit to drive Gran to the beauty parlor in Fairfield, where they wash her hair. Otherwise he has little to do.

Slight, white-haired Sylvie bustles around him, cooking a large, full lunch, which will appear in doll-sized portions on Gran's tray and return barely touched. Gran likes only toast now. Sylvie looks out past the screened kitchen door.

"Mrs. Fraser'll kill me if she sees what I've let grow." A patch of scraggly Scottish thistle has sprouted by the path, some of the purple blossoms dried to straw color.

"Oh, those sorry-looking weeds?" George is past fifty now, still with Irish in his voice as he kids the housekeeper.

"I told Carl not to cut them. Have you seen the finches they've brought round?"

"Oh, yes, and me without my gun."

"Oh, stop you. . . . They're yellow finches, the most beautiful little birds. Just this long . . ." She spreads her fingers four inches.

"Too small to roast. Good in a pie?"

A pause. Sylvie, slicing potatoes, says, "Yesterday she

224

asked if Miss Helen's called, when she's going to come by."

"I know."

"I told her that Miss Helen said she couldn't come round right now but wanted her to know that everything's fine."

"You're a good woman, Sylvie."

And so they go on, letting the thistles grow.

FELICITY

Seattle, Washington

For months after Helen died, Guinness would lie on Felicity's foot. Felicity would be sitting at her desk or sprawled in a chair, and the dog would place a paw on her foot, anchoring her companionably, securely—a weight that said "Don't go."

—

Tonight Felicity writes, by strong lamplight:

Dear Meredith—

Thanks for the letter. Yes, it's true. I'm back in school—summer classes, premed. And yes, UW's vet school is good, but we'll talk about that in six years.

Hugh bought me a desk lamp (high romance, I know).

We've gotten into a routine. I'll be studying and it will have gotten dark and I won't have noticed, I'll just hunch closer over the book. He'll come home from swimming—I won't even hear him—and he'll switch on my light. It's

(He just looked over my shoulder. I shooed him away, told him to do his own work. He says Hello.)

It's nice, Meredith. Him coming home in his grey sweatshirt, all warm and dry and smelling of chlorine. He always makes a pot of tea before going to his desk to correct papers. It's this way every night. And outside there's a steady rain. God, it's nice.

You asked about the stables.

I don't know if I told you this, but I spent a weekend out here last summer. Beautiful clear days walking the docks, watching the fishermen come in. But I was moping. I felt guilty about leaving the beasties for four days, thought no one could run that stable but me. And of course there was Mum.

So I basically gloom up the place, look sour and snap, until Hugh takes me by my arm and says:

"Look. You can pack and go back tonight and I promise I won't be mad. Now will you please be happy?"

"Happiness isn't the issue."

That night on the plane I thought about what I'd said, sat up all night under those rented headphones. Sat there feeling stupid.

People like you and I are responsible for their own happiness. If we're not, we have no one to blame but ourselves. That's the scary part. Choosing what out of all the options in the world will make us happy. (Note that I said options, not things. Meredith, I don't mean to be preachy, but keep that in mind.) Looking back, there's something obscene about being ungrateful.

So that's why I gave up the stables. I proved I could

work hard and make it a success, but I no longer wanted to be a slave to the beasties. I didn't enjoy it. I know that sounds like I've used financial freedom as an escape hatch, like our mothers did. But I think a lot depends on what you're escaping to. (Who was it that said, "When God closes a window he opens a door"? Yikes—I think it's from Sound of Music. *I better get back to Orgo before my mind turns completely to glue.)*

It's strange when you find things going better than planned. Hope they are for you too.

Take care, Meredith. And take care of Pearce, if possible. Sometimes it isn't, you know—

Love,

F.

———

Later that night:

Hugh rolls away at the feather caress of her hand, sleepily saying, "That tickles." They lie apart for a moment, gazing up at the ceiling, the striped cotton sheets bathed in the silver-blue light from the streetlamp, everything so clear for two o'clock in the morning. The radio's sleep timer clicks, shutting off the Springsteen song that's been on low.

Felicity feels the sheets stir around her legs, smooth and cool. With a slow rustle they slide down but not off. A warm weight falls firmly across her right ankle. Hugh's foot is hooked over hers, still and heavy and certain. She could not move it if she wanted to.

She reaches her hand back and finds his waist while he sleeps. She does not tickle. She just lets her hand rest. It is so quiet she can hear Guinness on the floor, breathing evenly, peacefully.

I am only one-half Mum, she thinks, maybe not even

that. And a baby would be one-half Hugh. The idea makes her happy.

She can see through the window from where she's lying. The blind is open, the streetlamp just beyond. She squints, as Hugh said she should.

Hugh was right. If she squinted hard and long, the streetlamp would become round and full as the moon.

PEARCE

Maine

If any of his friends had been on the island, they'd have said he brought the bad weather with him. He stood in the doorway to the back porch, watching a steady rain fall beyond the high columns. Out across the wet lawns lay an all-encompassing grey. The air was cold, the dampness inescapable, the sound of the rain drowning all others. It was this monochromatic, still quality that made the island either soothing or unbearable, depending on one's mood. As grey waves swept up over the rocks, Pearce considered his options.

Lulu would not be able to telephone—the phone company was typically late in reconnecting his service. The rain had, he feared, grounded the Cessna that he had hired to bring her and the Lowes up from Boston. The prospect of an evening alone on the quiet island frightened him; he had, for the past nine months, arranged to spend very little time either alone or quiet.

It had been an all-night drive up to Maine to catch the morning ferry. He didn't mind driving at night, since he didn't sleep well anyway. At night, in his new Porsche, he could pass other cars, or stop for gas or coffee, while in bed he'd wake suddenly, hot and cold, his heart beating fast, trying to lie still until morning.

Stella had come and opened the house several days before his arrival. Most everything appeared the same. This in particular bothered him.

It was getting dark—night coming early because of the rain. He wondered who else might be back. Lately he'd had plenty of people with whom to spend the dark hours. In New York, not sleeping was considered normal, even admirable. In Florida, he'd kept days busy with tennis and golf, cultivating a small reliable group of women, bartenders, and tennis pros for late-night parties at his house.

Cursing the phone company, he turned on the television. Not able to get a picture because of the weather, he left it on anyway, listening to commercials through static while flipping magazine pages.

Within minutes, the electricity went out. It happened often in a storm. He remembered nights from when he was small, how his mother would entertain him during blackouts to keep him from panicking. One night, by candlelight, she had taken a yellow snapdragon from the vase in the study. She had shown him how to hold and squeeze the flower, making it "snap." He had seen the imaginary dragon face easily enough; it had made him laugh. Later that night he woke from dragon nightmares. Large ones had crept up from the garden, up through the mist and rain, and crouched by his bedside. He cried loudly for his mother, and she came to him, saying that it was all right, that she sometimes dreamt of dragons too.

The Inn, he thought, The Inn might have electricity. It was on the other side of the island. There should be a few people and perhaps light. He grabbed his keys and ran out to where his car sat, black and shiny with rain.

The headlights flipped up to light a narrow corridor ahead as he sped toward town. The wooded road seemed narrower than before—the pines looming taller and closer, his seat lower and smaller. In this new car he could really feel the pavement, sense the speed at which it raced behind, underneath the wheels. It occurred to him that he was in complete control of the steering wheel, that he was its master. He had but to turn the wheel just an inch to either side, he thought, and one ton of complex machinery would respond, willingly. He and the car were moving so quickly that it would take less than a second. All he had to do was move his wrist an inch to the right and he'd be off . . . just that much. He stared down at his knuckles, feeling his joints ache and cramp under the tight grip with which he held the wheel. One inch . . .

His head jerked up suddenly as he felt the wheels lose the wet road. His hold on the steering wheel didn't help as the car skidded over the long puddle, then spun out wildly. Two seconds stretched long as he fought for control, pulling the car back to center as he came into a turn. Regaining the feel of the pavement, he handled the turn, then let up on the gas, gradually slowing the car to a crawl with the utmost concentration. Carefully, he pulled to the side of the road and clicked on the hazard lights. He did not feel anything as he stepped out; shock, perhaps. He did not know how long he spent there, standing by the roadside. He did not know his tremendous relief until he began to feel the rain on his shoulders like tiny hands. The drops first touched only his skin, a pleasing cool sensation. Soon they reached a deeper level of thick, knotted muscle. He felt the rain knead and pound his neck and shoulders, he felt his head and arms drop down, tired and grateful. He could not think when he'd last felt pleasure such as this.

He drove back to the house slowly, with deliberate care. The rain was letting up. In the dark, with the headlights on, he could see only the very edge of the woods. If his dragons still crouched there, they slept.

He pulled into the driveway and stepped out of the car. With both hands, he lifted the garage door. It rolled back easily. He drove the car in and switched off the engine. He pulled the door closed as he left, shivering slightly. Only then did he remember that his clothes were soaked through.

The electricity was back on. Grasping the heavy banister, he slowly climbed the stairs to his room. Stripping off his wet clothes, leaving them in a pile on the floor, he crawled under the down comforter. Seconds after turning off his bedside lamp, he fell into the first sound sleep he'd had for months.

MEREDITH

Heyton Hall, South Carolina

       I'm without a car. Willy picks me up in town.

"You like Beaufort?" he asks.

"I think so."

"You got a job here?"

"Yes, with the paper."

"Oh, that sounds real interestin'."

"Yes, it is. It really is."

We pass the entrance to the long driveway, the allée of oaks. From the road I can see that the rye grass is brown; the lawn won't be seeded until fall.

234

"Not too pretty now," says Willy.

"But it is."

Willy drops me at the old caretaker's cottage, near the stables. Bonnie barks from the doorway.

Uncle Linc appears beside her. "Hello, hello," he calls.

Linc resigned from his firm this past winter, took the caretaker's cottage for his own. He shows me around his place.

He lives mostly in the kitchen.

"Got a satellite dish now," Linc says, pointing to the twenty-inch TV on the checked plastic tablecloth.

There's mud tracked across the floor, tools and electrical parts spread along the counter.

"You hungry?"

"Thanks. I'm O.K. for now."

He takes a foil-covered bowl from the refrigerator. "Remember Chessy? I'd take her birds last winter. You know, for her. But when she'd cook 'em up, she'd bring some back for me. Treated me real good."

The refrigerator is stacked with covered platters, plastic freezer tubs.

"She's still bringin' these dishes of green beans, okra, sayin' now"—Linc imitates her, falsetto—" 'Mr. Linc! You eat somethin' green or I won't bring you youh cornbread.' " Then, voice lower: "Bonnie, you *love* vegetables, don'tcha, girl?" He feeds her greens by hand, letting her lick his fingers.

Everyone needs taking care of.

Linc shows me the quail pens, where the brood hens sit. We walk and talk.

"Any plans for Maine?"

"No. I don't get vacation time for a while."

"Summer's off-season. When I retired, people thought it was strange, me comin' down here. Well, I tell 'em I am strange."

"Then I'm strange, too."

Linc smiles. "Come on, I'll show you the shop." We walk down to the tin-roofed garage. To the left, a 1964 Mustang, its hood up. Mechanical parts litter a table, used rags on the floor.

Mostly, now, Linc tinkers with old tractors.

"They'll still run, if you just treat 'em right."

I see something familiar in one corner, something from a photograph. A set of hooded headlights on wooden slats.

"The Redbugs," he says. "I was in the bin when Mum sold Broadhurst. But Darcy was smart and sent all four down here. Been in storage. Rewired that one, got it running for a while. Gonna replace the battery on the other, wax the wood."

Before walking out, we stand for a moment, looking back at the electric cars.

"Neat, aren't they?" says Linc.

"Yes, they are."

And I think Linc was as happy as I to see that the other cared, that something was saved.

I was leasing a Thunderbird until Linc said, "Why don't you take my Buick?" That's the reason for today's trip, to pick up the car.

He shows me the ten-year-old Skylark, sky blue. "It'll get you where you need to go."

I get in, look to the gearbox, dismayed. "I don't know how to drive a stick."

"So we'll teach you." Linc hops in; Bonnie too.

We start, slowly, down the clay road, then turn onto the drive.

Halfway down the colonnade, I see that an oak is missing, sawed off to a stump.

"What happened?" I ask.

"Big storm last year. Tried to save it. No way."

But there was something grand to that stump, that gaping hole in the ranks. That tree had stood for two hundred years, had weathered storms. And now it was missed.

We continue up the drive, changing gears, shifting down.

About the Author

Marina Rust was born in Washington, D.C., and is a graduate of Duke University.